# Visions
# Coffe
# Maddie Goodwell 2

By

Jinty James

ISBN-13:978-1981409280

ISBN-10:1981409289

Please note: This book was formerly called Cappuccino Corpse

# CHAPTER 1

"I can't believe that in two days' time, this square is going to be transformed into a coffee festival!" Suzanne Taylor plopped onto a stool, wiggling her feet, as she sipped a vanilla cappuccino. Her blue eyes sparkled with enthusiasm, while her strawberry-blonde hair swung from side to side in a ponytail.

"I know," Maddie Goodwell agreed, looking out onto Estherville's town square. Smooth green lawn, with a few benches dotted here and there, would soon be turned into a bustling hive of activity – as well as providing an influx of visitors to the small township, located one hundred miles from Seattle.

"Mrrow." Trixie, the Persian cat, joined in the conversation. White and fluffy with a silver spine and tail, the feline's turquoise eyes looked lively with expectation.

Maddie and Suzanne had just recovered from the morning rush. Ever since they'd opened Brewed from the Bean seven months ago, their coffee truck had been a success. They were allowed to park at the town square, snagging joggers, office workers, and shoppers as their clientele.

And now, their truck was in prime position for the inaugural regional coffee festival.

Since coffee was Washington State's official drink, the town council had come up with an idea for a one-day festival, in conjunction with Aunt Winifred, a small town half an hour's drive away, and other townships nearby. And, to entice baristas to enter, there would be a competition for the best freshly made cappuccino. The prize was a wildcard entry into the state barista championship held in Seattle the following month.

"You're a shoo-in to win," Suzanne declared, taking another sip of her cappuccino.

"Do you think so?" Maddie furrowed her brow. "There are going to be other baristas here, not just Claudine from the coffee shop."

"Don't mention her name." Suzanne shuddered dramatically. "I don't even know why she bothered to enter. She has no chance!"

Claudine Claxton, the curmudgeonly coffee shop owner, was Maddie's nemesis. When the older woman had bought the coffee shop, Maddie's working conditions had become intolerable, until she finally quit her job, and started Brewed from the Bean with Suzanne, her best friend since middle school – and Trixie, of course.

Maddie made the coffee drinks and Suzanne handled the register and their new, profitable line of tempting morsels: health balls, made from a mixture of cacao, dates, coconut, and other wholesome ingredients. Trixie dozed on her stool, and occasionally greeted her favorite customers – when she wasn't busy grooming herself to maintain her pristine white and silver fur.

"You never know what a judge prefers," Maddie said, trying to be fair.

"I know he won't prefer her coffee over yours," Suzanne declared.

Most people who tried Claudine's coffee never went back for a second cup. Instead, they visited Brewed from the

Bean, telling Maddie how much they loved her coffee. It was amazing Claudine was still in business – somehow, the coffee shop owner was blinkered when it came to the art of making a good cup of espresso, informing everyone her coffee was wonderful, when it actually tasted like cheap swill.

"Mrrow!" Trixie agreed.

Maddie sank down on the stool next to Suzanne, nursing a vanilla latte. "Thanks, Trixie." She stroked the fluffy feline. "And you too, Suze."

Suzanne grinned. "If you add your signature art to the cappuccino, they'll be even more blown away."

"The rules don't state that cappuccino art is expected." Maddie frowned.

"But they don't say you can't do it," Suzanne pointed out. "And when you win, you'll get to compete in the big championship next month. Add Trixie's image to your microfoam, and we'll be packing our bags for Seattle!"

Trixie bunted Maddie's hand, as if nodding in agreement.

"Okay." Maddie crinkled her eyes. "You two are bossy!"

"Yeah." Suzanne grinned.

"Mrrow!"

They sat in silence for a couple of minutes, Maddie sipping her latte, and Suzanne finishing her cappuccino. Trixie continued to look out of the serving hatch, as if she could already see the town square being transformed into a coffee festival.

"Have you tried the Coffee Vision spell today?" Suzanne spoke.

"No." Maddie shook head.

"Broomf!" Trixie sounded disappointed.

"I haven't had time." Maddie sighed.

When she was seven, Maddie had stumbled across a crumbling old book called *Wytchcraft for the Chosen* in the local secondhand bookshop. She paid the one dollar the bookshop owner insisted was the price just for her, and sneaked it home, certain her conservative parents would not approve.

One spell in particular caught her attention – how to tell someone's future for the next twenty-four hours with the aid of a cup of coffee. When she used her own cup of coffee, she caught a glimpse of her future for the next day. When she cast the spell over a customer's cup of coffee, she could peek into their future over the next twenty-four hours.

Until recently, it was the only spell she could master from the dusty tome, despite a page in the book that stated a witch came into her full powers once she was seven-and-twenty. Maddie's twenty-seventh birthday had been several weeks ago…

Last month, she saw a vision – the murder of one of her regular customers! She, Trixie, and Suzanne had helped solve that murder, and along the way, she'd been able to cast a truth spell with success.

Maddie just hoped there wouldn't be any more murders in *her* future.

"Do it now." Suzanne nudged her.

"I'm not sure it will work." Maddie looked doubtfully at her latte. "I made this five minutes ago, and I've always cast it on a freshly made coffee."

"Try it," her friend urged.

Trixie looked at her expectantly, as if agreeing with Suzanne.

"Okay."

An image of a dark, handsome man standing outside their truck appeared.

"Really?" Maddie frowned.

"What do you see?" Suzanne peered over her shoulder, then slumped back. "I can't see anything."

"Ramon."

"No way!" Suzanne grinned. "Is he coming over here?"

"Yes." Maddie wasn't sure how she felt about her vision. Ramon was a sexy masseuse who owned a salon squeezed into a corner of the town square. She'd first met him last month, when she'd been investigating her customer's murder, although he hadn't been involved in that crime.

"I've got to get a massage from him." A dreamy look appeared on Suzanne's face.

"You mean you haven't already?" Maddie teased. Ever since she'd told Suzanne about Ramon, her friend had threatened to book a session with him.

"Not yet." Suzanne waved a hand around the truck. "We've been pretty busy."

"I know."

"Which is a good thing," Suzanne said in a cheery voice. "And I bet after the festival, business will be even better."

Before Maddie could reply, a tall, dark, handsome man – just like the cliché – appeared at the truck serving window, wearing dark chinos and a navy shirt.

"Hello, Maddie and Suzanne. And Trixie." Ramon smiled at them. His liquid brown eyes were framed with thick dark lashes, perfectly complementing his olive skin and firm, sensual lips.

Maddie waited a second for her breath to return to her lungs.

"Hi, Ramon." She hoped her voice didn't sound squeaky.

"Hi Ramon." Suzanne hopped over to the counter, returning his smile.

Trixie blinked up at him, her turquoise eyes bright and lively.

"You will be at the coffee festival?" he asked.

"Yes," they both answered breathlessly.

"Mrrow!"

"I will be there also." His faint Spanish accent made whatever he said sound impressive, even if he talked about mundane matters.

"Great." Suzanne grinned at him.

"You have not booked your massages with me." He crooked a finger at them. "Now I have sampled your coffee, Maddie, it is only right you and Suzanne sample me."

Maddie's cheeks heated, even though she knew he meant a strictly professional massage, and not – not him. In a romantic sense. Besides, he was too old for her – too old for both of them. She and Suzanne were twenty-seven and Ramon looked to be in his early forties.

"Yes." Suzanne's eyes gleamed with a hint of sexy. "We should definitely make an appointment with you right now."

Ramon nodded, digging into his pocket and bringing out his phone. "Let me see." He tapped the screen. "Yes, I am available this afternoon. Otherwise—" he looked up at them, "—it will have to be after the festival."

"That's fine," Maddie said quickly. She didn't know if she was ready for a massage with him. Just the thought of his large, tanned hands rubbing her shoulders – or her back – caused her stomach to flutter. And it was ridiculous. But there was just something about him – something so purely male and sensual – that made her feel that way. And by the way Suzanne was eyeing him, it seemed he had the same effect on her, too.

"I can make it this afternoon." Suzanne jumped in. She turned to Maddie. "Can't I?"

"Sure." Maddie nodded. "I'll be able to handle the customers."

"Good." Ramon tapped the screen again. "Two o'clock, Suzanne. Does that work for you?"

"Yes," she answered, her cheeks pink.

"And now, Maddie, if you will make me one of your delicious coffees, I shall be on my way." He turned and gestured to the couple of people standing behind him. "I am holding up your customers."

Maddie made his usual, an espresso, and handed it to him. He paid Suzanne and with a wave, walked across the square to his storefront.

"Phew!" Suzanne sipped from a bottle of water once they'd served the customers. "Am I ready to get a massage?"

"You've been talking of nothing else for the last few weeks," Maddie pointed out with a smile. "Go for it."

"Maybe I shouldn't leave you on your own with the festival only two days away." Suzanne frowned.

"There's not much to do," Maddie replied. "We're lucky we've got all our equipment here in the truck. The other stall holders will have to bring everything with them and set up. And I made sure to order extra beans, cups, and napkins when we first found out about it. I'll be fine on my own this afternoon."

"Okay," Suzanne said breathlessly, pulling off her hair elastic, finger-combing her locks, and pulling them back into a slightly neater ponytail. "How do I look?"

Before Maddie could answer, a whining, nasal voice assaulted their ears.

"No customers?" A stout forty-something woman with jet-black hair cropped short smirked at them.

Claudine.

"We're recovering from the morning rush," Suzanne said loftily, drawing herself to her full height of five foot six. "What can we do for you, Claudine?"

"Just checking to see if you girls are ready for the competition." Claudine's greedy gaze roamed over their coffee truck. "The press and the local radio station are going to cover the event. My café is sure to be featured in the newspaper, and I bet Dave Dantzler from the radio station will want me to be on his show. Expect to see me compete in the big competition in Seattle next month, girls."

Suzanne snorted. "I don't think so. Everyone knows Maddie will win. And I'm sure the paper will feature all the contestants equally. As will Dave Dantzler."

"Don't count your coffee beans before they're roasted." Claudine shook her finger at both of them.

"As if she knows anything about roasting beans," Suzanne muttered under her breath to Maddie.

Maddie silently agreed. From her time working at the curmudgeon's café, she knew Claudine would be happy to serve instant coffee and call it freshly brewed espresso if she could get away with it. That was one of the reasons Maddie had quit.

"Been practicing your cappuccino art?" Suzanne asked.

"What?" Claudine's eyes widened.

"Art is allowed on top of the cappuccino," Maddie said.

"Art?" Claudine glowered.

"You know, hearts, flowers, words," Suzanne informed her.

A vein throbbed in Claudine's temple. "Why was I not informed of this?"

"It's in the rules." Suzanne shrugged. "Haven't you read them?"

"The rules do not say art is allowed on the cappuccino," Claudine huffed.

"But it doesn't say it's disallowed," Maddie said gently, realizing she was echoing what Suzanne had told her earlier.

"But – but—" Claudine stared at them, no longer looking smug.

Maddie even felt sorry for her.

"You better go and practice, then." Suzanne waved her hand.

"Oh – oh – oof!" Claudine spun around and stalked off toward her café on the other side of the square.

"Don't you think you were a little hard on her?" Maddie asked once Claudine was out of earshot.

"Nope." Suzanne shrugged. "I know how horrible she was to you when you worked for her – she deserves a little payback. Besides, we probably did her a favor without realizing it. Now she'll practice and not feel left out that she was the only one without art on her cappuccino entry."

"But ... words?" Maddie tried to suppress a giggle. "I haven't attempted words for my coffee art."

"You don't need to," Suzanne said loyally. "Your picture of Trixie is what every other barista wishes they could do. I'm sure you're going to win the competition."

***

Just after three o'clock, Suzanne came back to the truck.

"Well?" Maddie studied her friend, who looked flushed and had a faraway look in her eye. "How was the massage?"

"It was amazing!" Suzanne gushed. "Totally professional and legit – but his voice – oh, Mads – his voice sent delicious shivers down my spine the whole time." She looked dreamily into the distance. "I swear Mads, I'm going to marry that man one day."

Maddie smiled. Suzanne frequently got enthusiastic about certain things – like nagging Maddie about creating health balls as another profit stream – and she usually persisted until she turned the vision in her head into reality. But Maddie couldn't decide whether Suzanne was serious about marrying Ramon one day or she'd just gotten carried away by the massage.

"I wonder why he's not married already?" Maddie said thoughtfully. "Or at least spoken for." She glanced at her friend. “Maybe there is someone in his life.”

“He doesn’t wear a ring and I didn’t see any photos in his office,” Suzanne said. “Maybe he just doesn’t want to break the heart of every woman in the world by marrying.”

“Apart from the woman he marries,” Maddie pointed out.

“Which would be me.” Suzanne pointed to herself, grinning.

At this point, Trixie decided to make a contribution to the conversation.

“Mrrow!”

“You can be one of my bridesmaids, too, Trixie.” Suzanne looked at Maddie and they both burst out laughing. Unfortunately, Trixie didn’t look like she appreciated the joke.

“Sorry, Trix.” Suzanne gently stroked the fluffy white cat until she purred, the feline’s turquoise eyes ecstatically narrowing to slits. “We weren’t laughing at you.”

The cat bunted Suzanne’s hand, as if accepting her apology.

"I swear Trixie understands what we're talking about." Suzanne shook her head in wonder.

"I know," Maddie said.

"Are you going to bring her to the festival?"

"I thought it might be better if she stays at home, but—" Maddie studied her cat's face, which now seemed to be on the verge of pouting "—she can come if she wants to."

"Mrrow!" Trixie purred and pushed her head against Maddie's hand, demanding to be petted.

"All right." Maddie sighed. "You can come to the festival, Trixie."

## CHAPTER 2

Saturday, the day of the festival, dawned bright and clear. The sun shone in the light blue sky, hinting at a perfect Spring day.

Trixie had woken Maddie up at six a.m., insisting on being fed *right now.*

Maddie stared at her bowl of breakfast cereal, her stomach too jumbled with nerves to make eating feasible. She resisted making a latte for herself, worried the caffeine would make her even more on edge.

Why had she entered the competition?

It hadn't even been Suzanne's idea. Or Trixie's. It had been hers alone.

She was good at pulling a shot of espresso. More than good at it. But she didn't need to win a small town competition to tell her that.

Or a big state one.

She had thought entering the contest, rather than just taking part in the festival, would be good for business.

But now she wasn't so sure.

"Mrrow!" Trixie called from the living room.

Maddie hurried into the room, wondering what the cat was up to.

The Persian sat hunched over *Wytchcraft for the Chosen.*

"What is it, Trix?" Maddie asked.

"Mrrow." The cat gently touched the cover of the book with her paw.

"I'm not going to look for a spell to find out how to win the competition," she informed Trixie. Last night, when she'd tossed and turned trying to fall asleep, she'd wondered if there was such a spell in the book. Then instantly told herself not to think about it, because it would be cheating. And she was not a cheat.

She'd had the magical book for twenty years and had studied each page thoroughly during that time. She couldn't remember such a spell, and even if there was one, so far she could only manage the Coffee Vision spell and the Tell the Truth enchantment.

Some witch she was.

Although the book didn't say anything about the rule of three – that what you did, either good or bad, would come back to you threefold – she knew enough from watching TV shows and movies over the years that using magic for your own personal gain *was not a good idea.* Even if those TV shows and movies were fiction, surely there was a grain of truth to that belief?

"Mrrow." Trixie looked disappointed.

"If I can't win without magic, then it wasn't meant to be."

The cat stared at her with her gleaming turquoise eyes, then seemed to accept the statement.

"M …r…r…o…w."

"I'm glad you understand." Maddie smiled. She was also glad nobody was witnessing the conversation. They might think she was totally mad, the way she spoke to Trixie, as if the Persian could understand her, but Maddie was sure she could – when she wanted to.

One year ago, Trixie had wandered into the coffee shop, sat on the floor beneath the counter and looked up at Maddie.

"Mrrow."

"Are you lost?" Maddie stepped from around the coffee machine and bent down.

"Mrrow."

She could have sworn that had sounded like "No."

Claudine, the new owner, came out from the back and had started shouting, "Get that animal out, or else!"

Instinctively, Maddie scooped up the feline and hurried outside, turning back to scowl at her boss, before carrying the pretty cat home.

"You can stay with me until I find your owner," Maddie had whispered, soft white fur tickling her fingers. The cat nestled in her arms, as if there was nowhere else she'd rather be.

As Maddie hurried back to work, she shook off the ridiculous thought that the Persian had been trying to tell her that she belonged to Maddie.

No one had claimed her, and now Trixie was a big part of Maddie's life, including being interested in *Wytchcraft for the Chosen.* Did that mean Trixie was Maddie's familiar?

"We've got to get ready for the festival."

Trixie jumped off the sofa and trotted toward Maddie's bedroom, stopping and looking back at Maddie as if to say, "Come on!"

***

Rock music blared from the speakers set in the town square. The space was buzzing with people, stalls – and coffee.

The rich smell of freshly pulled espresso, combined with chocolate and cinnamon, wafted throughout the outdoor area.

Maddie wore jeans and a plum wrap top that she thought went well with her brown hair and amber eyes, while Suzanne also wore jeans with a pastel blue long-sleeved top that emphasized her fair coloring.

"I'm so nervous," Maddie confessed to Suzanne. They sat on stools inside the truck, Trixie next to them.

"So am I, even though I'm not competing," Suzanne replied. "I don't think Trixie is, though."

"No." Maddie glanced at the cat. Her eyes were alive with interest as she stared at the scene on the other side of the truck's serving window. She didn't seem anxious at all.

Although it was only nine o'clock, they'd already served some customers. Today was going to be good for business, even if she didn't win the cappuccino making contest.

"You should try your competitor's coffee," Suzanne urged. "See if it's any good."

"Maybe later," Maddie replied. The last thing she needed was to have her nerves any more jangled.

"When's the judging happening?" Suzanne asked.

"Any time between ten and eleven." Maddie read through the information sheet. "The judge, Edward Grenville, will be here, accompanied by a newspaper reporter and the radio personality, who will give me a quick interview. Then I make my entry, with the judge watching, and this is where I get to tell him about the coffee I'm serving him. The winner will be announced this afternoon."

"One hour to go." Suzanne smiled sympathetically.

Before Maddie could answer, an elderly couple walked up to the counter, both asking for a cappuccino.

"Just like you'll be making in the competition." The woman grinned.

Although Maddie didn't know them, she smiled back, and started making the drinks, adding her signature art of Trixie to the top of the microfoam.

"That is so cute," the woman gushed. "Look, Hank, it's a cat!"

Her husband took a sip of his drink, his eyes widening in appreciation. "This is good."

"Oh, is that your cat?" The woman gestured to Trixie, sitting on a stool inside the truck.

"Yes," Maddie said. "Her name is Trixie."

"She's gorgeous." The woman's gaze travelled from the cappuccino art on her drink to Trixie and back again. "Such a good likeness."

"Thank you," Maddie replied, pride blossoming inside her. She wasn't much of an artist with pen and paper, but somehow she was able to create art on microfoam.

"Mmm, this is delicious." The woman tasted her cappuccino. "I hope you win the competition."

"Thanks," Maddie and Suzanne spoke at the same time.

"Would you like to try a health ball?" Suzanne gestured to the small samples rolled in shredded coconut and arranged attractively on a white plate. "Everyone loves them."

"Why not?" The woman smiled. She plucked one from the plate, popped it in her mouth and chewed. Delight flickered across her face. "Hank, we've got to get some of these!"

After buying four health balls and cooing over Trixie some more, the couple finally left, sipping their cappuccinos.

"That went well," Suzanne said with satisfaction, rearranging the sample plate on the counter.

"Mrrow," Trixie agreed.

Maddie grabbed a bottle of water from the small fridge and gulped some down. Since she'd sworn off coffee until after she competed, perhaps a mouthful of cool water would help calm her. But her stomach was still tied up in knots.

"Hi." A plump, jolly looking woman with frizzy blonde hair came up to the counter. "I'm Jill from Aunt Winifred. My stall's over there." She gestured to a white tent opposite Maddie's truck. A wooden serving table occupied the space, complete with an espresso machine. Dried flowers decorated the front of the stall.

"I guess you're entered in the competition too?" she asked.

"Yes. I'm Maddie." Maddie replied, instantly liking the other woman. She looked to be in her forties, with rosy cheeks and laughter lines around her eyes. "And this is Suzanne." She gestured to her friend. "And Trixie."

"Mrrow," Trixie said politely, studying the woman.

"Oh, wow, you're allowed to bring your cat with you? I have a big boisterous dog but I left him at home. I didn't want him to wreck the place."

"No one's ever complained about Trixie being in the truck," Maddie said carefully, wondering if Jill was thinking of complaining.

"That's cool." Jill grinned. "I just wanted to say good luck in the competition. May the best barista win. And if you're ever passing Aunt Winifred, stop in at my cafe for a coffee – on the house."

"Thanks." Suzanne's eyes lit up. "Same to you. And please, take a free sample of our health balls." She held out the plate to Jill.

"Don't mind if I do." Jill picked up a coconut crusted ball and popped it in her mouth. "Yum!"

"We think so." Suzanne grinned. "Our customers love them."

"Now you've got me thinking." A faraway look entered Jill's blue eyes. "I'm going to try making those myself when I get home. Is that okay?" She furrowed her brow.

"Go for it." Suzanne gestured to the sample plate. "This is my secret recipe, but I made our first batch from a recipe I found online. There are tons of variations. And they made us a profit from day one."

"Good to know." Jill smiled, and then turned toward her stall. "I better get back before the judging starts!" With a friendly wave, she headed back toward her stall.

"I like her." Maddie sipped more water. Now her mouth was dry. More nerves?

"Yep," Suzanne agreed. "And her dog sounds like fun. Hey, why don't we go to Aunt Winifred one day and check out her café? Free coffee!"

"Good idea," Maddie agreed. "What about next week?"

They settled on Tuesday, deciding to give themselves an extra day off.

"She might be closed on Monday," Suzanne said.

"Or recovering from today," Maddie added. It was only 9.30, but she was tired from all the excitement already.

She looked out at the scene. More and more people strolled on the lawn, stopping at each coffee stall and talking to the vendors.

And then, she saw him.

Maddie froze.

She told herself to act natural.

"Hi, Maddie." A tall, attractive guy with auburn hair came up to the counter. "How's it going?"

"Great, Luke." Maddie told herself to breathe. Suzanne's older brother stood right in front of her!

She'd had a schoolgirl crush on Luke ever since she'd met him, when she and Suzanne had been in middle school. But he'd always treated her as if she were just a friend of his sister's, nothing more.

Which she was, she'd told herself over the years.

But that didn't stop her noticing *him.*

He was two years older than Suzanne, and had helped them find and restore their truck that they'd named Brewed from the Bean seven months ago. She'd nursed a hope that he would finally see her in a different light – a romantic light. But he hadn't.

Maddie had resigned herself to the fact that her schoolgirl crush was to forever remain that way, when he showed up now, on the morning of the competition.

"What are you doing here, Luke?" Suzanne frowned.

Maddie had never confided her feelings to her best friend, not wanting Suzanne to disapprove or feel weird that Maddie had a crush on her brother. But she did know that Suzanne hadn't told her brother that Maddie was a witch – or that Maddie and Suzanne thought she was, anyway. If she could call herself a witch with only two spells under her belt.

"Giving you some moral support." He grinned, his teeth even and white.

Maddie suppressed a girly sigh.

Suzanne checked her watch. "The competition starts soon, and Maddie's already nervous."

"You are?" He looked at her sympathetically. "But the judging hasn't started yet, it's only me."

That was the problem, but there was no way Maddie was going to tell him that.

"Come back after the competition." Suzanne shooed him away.

"Only if you promise to make me a coffee later." He looked questioningly at Maddie.

She nodded, afraid if she spoke it would be a squeak.

"Okay, then." He snagged a health ball before Suzanne could smack away his hand, and strode across the green lawn.

Maddie turned to look at Suzanne with wide eyes. "You know?" she whispered.

"Uh-huh." Suzanne smiled sympathetically. "I would love it if you two got together. Then I wouldn't have to feel guilty about marrying Ramon."

They started giggling. Trixie looked like she was smiling.

"What do you think, Trixie?" Suzanne asked. "Do you think you'd like my brother as a step-dad?"

"Suzanne!" Maddie blushed furiously.

"I don't think he knows," Suzanne said. "Idiot. And don't worry, I haven't told him anything about – you know – the book or your Coffee Vision spell."

"I know," Maddie answered. Somehow, deep inside herself, she'd always known that Suzanne had kept her word and not told anyone else about *Wytchcraft for the Chosen,* or Maddie's ability to peek into someone's future for the next twenty-four hours.

"And speaking of *you know*," Suzanne kept her voice low, "have you thought about casting it today?"

"No." Maddie shook her head. Trying the Coffee Vision spell had been the last thing on her mind this morning.

"Don't you think you should? If you see yourself winning the competition, then you wouldn't be so nervous."

"But … wouldn't that be like cheating?" Maddie furrowed her brow.

"Mrrow," Trixie joined in.

Maddie wasn't sure if the cat agreed or disagreed with her stance.

"I just thought it might give you some added confidence. Not that you should need it," Suzanne said. "Honestly, Mads, your coffee is the best. Everyone says so. And I doubt any of these other people—" she waved a hand to encompass the stalls dotted over the green "—would be able to make cappuccino art as good as you. And even if they could, I bet they don't have a cute cat on their entry."

"But I don't want to win with a gimmick," Maddie replied. "I want to win because my cappuccino is the best."

"And it will be," Suzanne assured her. "But I bet presentation is one of the areas the judges will consider as well. I doubt a sloppy looking cappuccino, even if it tasted good, is going to win over a great looking *and* tasting cappuccino."

Before Maddie could reply, a couple in their fifties hurried over to the truck.

"Are we too late, honey?" The woman had dark brown hair touched with gray and a warm smile, and wore dove-gray slacks with a matching sweater. "Has the judge seen you yet?"

"Not yet, Mom." Maddie returned her mother's smile.

"Try not to be nervous, dear." Her mother patted her hand. "Oh, look, you brought Trixie."

"She insisted on coming," Maddie replied.

Her mother made a small tsking sound that Maddie interpreted to mean that she didn't believe that to be entirely true, but Maddie let it go. Growing up, she hadn't had pets, apart from a rabbit, and Trixie was her first cat, as well as her familiar – *perhaps.*

Maddie had never told her parents about *Wytchcraft for the Chosen,* certain her conservative parents would not approve. And she wasn't going to start now.

"Health ball, Mr. Goodwell?" Suzanne held out the sample plate.

"Thanks, Suzanne." Maddie's father chose one and started chewing. "Mmm." He dug out his wallet and held out some cash. "Give me two more."

"Peter," Maddie's mom said, "you'll ruin your appetite."

"I doubt any of the offerings at the other stalls will be as good as these." He held out one of the balls to his wife.

Maddie's mother put it in her mouth and elegantly chewed. "You're right," she admitted. "Suzanne, I don't know what you put in these things, but I'm convinced they're magic."

Maddie and Suzanne looked at each other. The irony was that there was no magic involved in Suzanne's healthy treats.

"We'll come back later for a cup of coffee, dear," her mother said. "You have a little rest before the judge arrives – sit on the stool next to Trixie until it's time to make the best cappuccino ever. Good luck!"

"Yes, Mom." Maddie followed her mother's orders, stroking Trixie as she sat next to the feline.

"I can make the coffees if we get any customers before the judging," Suzanne offered, once Maddie's parents left. While she was decent at making lattes and cappuccinos, she wasn't as good as Maddie.

"Thanks." Maddie smiled at her friend.

Before she had time to take a breath though, the nasal whine of her nemesis struck her ears.

"How's it going, girls?" Claudine propped her elbows on the truck counter.

Suzanne scowled and shooed at Claudine's arms. "This is for customers."

"Take it easy." Claudine smirked, slowly removing her elbows from the white counter. "Nervous, Maddie?"

Before Maddie could reply, Suzanne jumped in. "Why should she be nervous? Everyone knows she makes the best coffee for miles around."

"Keep telling yourself that." Claudine studied her inky black painted fingernails, then held them out. "I got my nails done especially for today. They look good, don't they?"

"Yes," Suzanne grudgingly admitted, "If you like that depressing color of black."

"Ha ha." Claudine did not look amused. "Anyway, I decided to stop by and wish you girls luck, because you're going to need it. I'm going to blow the judge away with my cappuccino and win the contest. And then all your customers will come to my café instead and you'll be begging me for a job." Her gaze flickered over both of them, dismissing Trixie. "Which I *might* give you, if you ask very nicely."

"In your dreams." Suzanne snorted.

"There is no way I will ever work for you again." Maddie found her voice.

"Mrrow!" Trixie said indignantly. Maddie thought the cat still remembered Claudine chasing her out of the café on the day they'd met.

"Your loss." Claudine shrugged.

"Hello, Maddie and Suzanne." Ramon's, rich, deep voice was a delight after Claudine's nasal whine. "And Trixie, of course."

"Hi Ramon." Suzanne blushed.

"Hi," Maddie murmured with a smile. Now that she'd seen Suzanne's brother Luke that morning, suddenly Ramon didn't seem quite as sexy. He still was, she knew that, but deep down inside herself, she wanted Luke, not Ramon.

"Mrrow." Trixie greeted the masseuse, a playful look on her face.

"Oh, Ramon." Claudine turned to him. "I'm Claudine and I own the café near your salon and I've heard you give *wonderful* massages." She positively gushed, her shrill voice making Maddie wince.

"Some people seem to think so," Ramon said, attempting to look modest.

"I must have one with you. I must!" Claudine's face was animated.

Maddie and Suzanne looked at each other, as if to say, "Yikes!"

"There is no way I would ever give that woman a massage," Suzanne whispered in Maddie's ear. "I'd rather eat dirt."

"Let me check my calendar." Ramon dug his phone out of his jeans pocket. He pressed some buttons. "Yes, I have one appointment left on Monday afternoon at four o'clock."

"I'll take it!" Claudine answered.

"You know where I am?"

Something that sounded like a cross between a giggle and a squeal emitted from Claudine's lips. "Everyone knows where *your* salon is, Ramon."

"OMG," Suzanne muttered to Maddie. "Is she trying to *flirt* with him?"

"Good. I will see you then, Claudine."

"Yes," Claudine breathed, looking at him longingly. Then, as if she finally realized where she was, her demeanor changed. "And I'll see *you* from the winner's podium, Maddie."

The older woman flounced away, Maddie wondering if her peculiar stride was another flirtation effort.

"I take it you are not friends with her?" Ramon asked curiously.

"No way." Suzanne shook her head vigorously, her ponytail swinging from side to side.

"No," Maddie replied. "She used to be my boss, until Suzanne and I struck out on our own."

"I think she is an unhappy woman," Ramon said. "Perhaps my massage will make her feel a little better. More relaxed."

"She's not a nice woman, Ramon," Suzanne told him. "She's always coming over to our truck, trying to cause trouble."

"Do not fear, Suzanne." Ramon patted Suzanne's hand. By the look on her face, Maddie thought her friend was trying not to swoon. "I have dealt with women like Claudine before. A little kindness can work wonders, as well as the right essential oils. Perhaps she will not bother you after her massage."

A moment later, Ramon left, wishing them the best of luck.

"I so want to marry that man," Suzanne declared, her gaze following him as he strolled to the other side of the green. "I mean, he's kind to awful old women like Claudine!"

"She's not that old," Maddie protested, wondering why she was even bothering to defend her nemesis. But she and Suzanne were twenty-seven and Claudine looked to be in her forties.

"You know what I mean, Mads," Suzanne replied. "Maybe not so much old in years, as in her outlook."

"You could be right," Maddie agreed.

"Mrrow!" Trixie joined in the conversation.

Just then, a flurry of activity nearby heralded the arrival of the judge.

"Here they come," whispered Suzanne, suddenly standing tall.

Maddie took a deep breath, telling herself not to be nervous. *This can't possibly be worse than working for Claudine.* At that bracing thought, she pinned a smile to her lips and looked out of the serving hatch.

"Ready, girls?" A short, overweight man in his fifties with a bristly brown beard and an oily smile approached them. He held a microphone toward them.

He was accompanied by a wiry looking man in his forties, who had receding dark hair and wore horn-rimmed glasses.

A third gentleman smiled at Maddie and Suzanne. He was older than the other two men and had an air of gravitas about him.

"I'm Edward Grenville, the judge for today," the eldest man spoke. "This is Dave Dantzler, from Mornings with Dantzler on KBJW, and Walt, the newspaper reporter from the Estherville Star. They'll be interviewing you after I judge your entry."

Maddie nodded, remembering reading something about that on the competition form.

Are you ready—" the judge looked down at the clipboard he held "—Maddie Goodwell?" He suddenly seemed to spot Trixie. "And who do we have here?" He smiled.

"This is Trixie," Maddie said, wondering if she'd get points taken off her entry or even disqualified for having a cat in the truck. Trixie's presence had never worried the health inspector, and

Maddie hadn't given a second thought that she might not be welcome today.

"Charming," the judge said. "And this business is Brewed from the Bean?"

"Yes," Suzanne spoke.

"Good." The judge made a notation on his form. "We just have to double check everything. It would be terrible if the wrong person won, because their stall wasn't where it was supposed to be."

Maddie smiled politely. Her stomach fizzed with nerves, and she took a deep breath.

As crazy as it seemed, somehow she could feel Trixie silently reaching out and offering her support. Feeling more centered, Maddie waited for the judge's instructions.

"I would like you to make me a cappuccino. I assume you've read the rules?"

"Yes, sir," Maddie replied.

"Good. The amount of time it takes you is also taken into account. However, I will primarily be judging on taste and appearance." He held up a stopwatch. "Your time starts now."

Maddie flew to the coffee machine, her movements a blur. She'd practiced in her spare time over the last week, although Suzanne had protested that surely she didn't need to train for the contest, when she made coffees all day long in the truck?

But a fierce kernel of competitive pride had made her want to win – she cared more about her own reputation and beating Claudine fair and square than she did about making it to the barista competition in Seattle.

The machine buzzed and whirred as she pulled what she hoped was a great tasting shot. She'd specifically chosen dark roasted Arabica beans for this competition – she often used the same kind of beans for her customers' drinks, and thought they would give her the best chance of success in the competition.

The aroma of the espresso shot filled the truck, sweet notes of fruity complexity, as Maddie steamed the milk. She could feel Suzanne and Trixie silently cheering her on. No longer nervous, Maddie confidently poured the milk into the cup, adding her signature art – a picture of Trixie.

Surreptitiously exhaling, she presented the cappuccino to the judge. Win or lose, she'd just made one of the best cappuccinos of her life!

The judge sniffed appreciatively, the other two men peering over his shoulder as he studied the cat art on top of the foam.

"Charming." He smiled, his gaze flickering to Trixie and back to his cup. "Yes." He made a note on his clipboard.

Maddie held her breath. Would he still think it was "charming" when he tasted the coffee?

He took a sip. She didn't know whether to close her eyes or keep watching him. Her curiosity won out, and she kept her gaze trained on him.

The judge's expression didn't give much away, but Maddie told herself surely she would know if he hated the taste of her cappuccino?

He looked down at the cup, and took another sip. And another. Finally, he stated his verdict. "Delicious, Ms. Goodwell."

Maddie breathed a sigh of relief. She turned to look at Suzanne, who had a huge grin on her face. Trixie looked pleased as well.

"Thank you, sir," Maddie said.

"We have one more contestant to go, and then I need to tabulate the scores. The winner will be announced later today."

Maddie sank down on the stool, not sure if her legs could still support her. She watched the judge head toward a small tent marked *Private* on the other side of the square.

"Don't get too comfy." Dave Dantzler, the overweight radio personality, smirked. "I'll be interviewing you first, and then Walt will, for the newspaper."

"Sure," Maddie replied, bristling at his tone. She noticed out of the corner of her eye that Trixie no longer looked relaxed, and instead sat up straight on her stool, as if determined to keep a stern eye on him.

"What's your secret to making a good cup of coffee?" Dave asked.

"Using the best ingredients possible."

"Such as?" The radio personality looked a little bored.

"Such as buying the best beans I can, ensuring they're roasted to bring out the greatest flavor, and using the highest quality milk and chocolate powder for the dusting on top of the cappuccino," Maddie replied evenly.

"Everyone loves Maddie's mochas," Suzanne put in. "It's partly because of the chocolate powder she uses, and she's not mean with it like some other baristas." A telltale roll of her eyes alerted Maddie to the fact that Suzanne was talking about Claudine.

"What's the other reason people *love* her mochas?" Dave asked, sounding like he was making fun of Suzanne's statement.

"The coffee," Maddie replied. "It all comes down to the quality of the coffee, and how you use it." She didn't like the tone this man was taking, but she was just relieved her part in the competition had finished. Besides, it was a regional radio station – how many listeners did this man have? His behavior was a tad obnoxious so far – did he sound like that on the air?

"Thanks—" Dave looked down at his notes "—Maddie Goodwell. I've got what I need." He looked at his colleague Walt, the newspaper reporter. "Your turn."

"Hi," the scrawny man said. Behind his horn-rimmed glasses his eyes gleamed with intelligence. "Do you mind if I record this?" He held up his phone.

Maddie and Suzanne looked at each other, then shook their heads. After all, Dave Dantzler had just recorded them for his show.

"How long have you been operating Brewed from the Bean?" Walt asked.

"Seven months," Maddie replied.

"And where do you normally park your truck? So our readers can check you out?" he added.

"Here." Suzanne jumped into the conversation. "This is our usual site and the organizers said we could keep it for the festival."

"That was fortunate. So, how do you think you went in the competition?"

"Um … I don't like to speculate," Maddie eventually replied. What could she say? That she hoped she was the winner? She didn't want to come off over-confident in her interview. If she didn't win, she'd look foolish.

"Maddie's coffee is awesome," Suzanne said. "You should put that in your article."

"Mm." The reporter looked like he was trying not to smile at Suzanne's enthusiasm. "And what about your cat? Does she come to work with you every day?"

"Not all the time," Maddie said cautiously. "Sometimes she likes taking a break at home."

"Mrrow," Trixie agreed.

"Her name is Trixie," Suzanne put in.

"She's certainly cute," the reporter commented. His gaze landed on the sample plate of health balls. "What are these?"

"Try one," Suzanne urged, holding the plate toward him. "These are my specialty, just like coffee is Maddie's. They're healthy but delicious."

"Hmm." The reporter chewed, then swallowed. "What do you call them? I'll include it in my article."

Suzanne's eyes lit up. "Health balls. They contain coconut, dates, and cacao – not cocoa."

"They're certainly tasty," the reporter agreed. "So what are your plans after the competition, Maddie? If you win the wild card entry into the big Seattle competition?"

"Maddie will compete, of course," Suzanne said before Maddie could open her mouth.

"That's right," Maddie added with a rueful smile. She loved Suzanne, but sometimes her best friend spoke for her.

"And after that?" the reporter probed.

"If she wins that competition, she'll be able to compete in the nationals," Suzanne said.

"Yes." Maddie wondered if the article would actually mention any of her comments or if it would only include Suzanne's statements.

"And what about Brewed from the Bean? Any plans to expand?"

"We haven't thought about that yet," Maddie jumped in. And it was true. For the moment, Maddie was quite happy running this truck with Suzanne and

Trixie. They made enough money to cover their living expenses plus some extra to invest in the business.

"But we hope to," Suzanne put in.

"Okay." The newspaper reporter nodded. "I think that's all for now." He craned his head toward the other side of the lawn. The judge emerged from the private tent, striding toward a stall opposite Maddie and Suzanne.

"Good luck," Walt said. "It looks like the judge is ready for the last contestant."

"Thank you," Maddie said.

"Mrrow," Trixie added.

"Phew!" Suzanne flopped onto a stool. "I'm glad it's all over – apart from having to wait until you're announced the winner!"

"So am I," Maddie said wryly. "And I mightn't win. You know that."

"Do not." Suzanne grinned. "Okay, I won't say it again but I reserve the right to say I told you so when they hand you the trophy."

"There's a trophy?"

Trixie's ears pricked.

"Yep." Suzanne winked. "I had a peek inside the judge's tent this morning when everyone was setting up. It's small but it's definitely a gold trophy."

"Suzanne!" Maddie didn't know whether to be shocked or amused. "What if you got caught? They might have disqualified me."

"I hadn't thought of that." Suzanne looked momentarily chagrined. "Sorry, Mads. I promise not to do something like that again."

"Good." Maddie blew out a breath. "Because if I do win—" she felt uncomfortable saying that out loud and hurried on, "—they might have security at the Seattle contest and if you tried to get a peek at the prizes there—"

"Don't worry," Suzanne hastened to reassure her. "I wouldn't blow your chances like that." She appeared to realize what she'd just said. "Okay, yeah, I shouldn't have succumbed to temptation this morning." She looked around as if checking for eavesdroppers but apart from passersby strolling through the green and stopping at the different stalls, there didn't seem to be anyone loitering. "Thank goodness nobody saw me." She lowered her voice.

"Thank goodness," Maddie echoed. Although she'd been trying to downplay it, she really wanted to win the competition.

"You stole my beans – you – you bean thief!" Claudine's shrill voice caught their attention.

# CHAPTER 3

"What …?" Maddie's eyes widened. She stared across the square to the stall the judge had just departed. Claudine's hands were on her hips and she glared at a short burly man with curly black hair.

"What are you talking about?" the man demanded.

"You have the same beans as me!"

"So?" He looked confused.

"My beans are one of a kind. Everybody says so!" Claudine looked like she was going to shriek with rage.

"Yeah, one of a kind awful," Suzanne muttered to Maddie.

Even Trixie seemed transfixed by the angry tableaux.

Dave Dantzler shoved his microphone in between the man and Claudine. "What's going on, guys? Talk to me."

"He stole my beans." Claudine's voice was loud enough for everyone at the festival to hear.

"I have no idea what this person is talking about." The coffee vendor seemed genuinely confused. His voice was also loud enough for Maddie to hear.

Claudine drew herself up and stuck out her chest. "I just happened to be passing after the judging, and I noticed that this – this *person* had the same beans as I did, and that the judge had just left. Naturally, I was concerned that this – this *person* stole my beans. I believe I have an extremely good chance of winning the competition and my beans are part of my success. And now – and now—" Claudine's face puckered.

"She really is delusional," Suzanne whispered to Maddie. "Her coffee is awful – not even adding chocolate powder and calling it a mocha can save it – I tested one at her café a few months ago, remember?"

"Yes." Maddie nodded. Suzanne hadn't been able to stop talking about how bad it had been.

"It's not against the rules for competitors to use the same kind of beans," Dave Dantzler put in.

"That's right." The newspaper reporter nodded.

"But … but …" Claudine seemed to deflate a little.

"I did not steal your beans," the coffee vendor defended himself. "Here, take a look for yourself." He gestured at his stall. "I doubt they're the same as yours – I get mine roasted from a small company just outside Seattle." He pulled out a bag from underneath his stall and thrust it at Claudine.

Claudine scanned the writing, first holding the bag close to her face and then further away, squinting at the writing.

"Do you think she needs glasses?" Maddie murmured to Suzanne.

"I think you're right." Suzanne looked at Maddie. "That's what Mom was doing before she got reading glasses."

"Well?" The radio personality waved his microphone in front of Claudine.

"Well …" Claudine hesitated, then took a deep breath. "I guess they're not the same after all. But the bag looks very similar to mine."

"How do you feel about being falsely accused of stealing?" Dave shoved his microphone toward the coffee vendor's face.

The man shrugged. “We all make mistakes. And I think everyone is anxiously waiting to find out who won.”

Claudine grudgingly handed back the bag of beans.

“That’s very decent of you,” Walt, the newspaper reporter, commented.

“Everyone likes having an edge in a competition,” the coffee vendor said. “I’m just glad she accused me *after* the judging.”

The three men laughed, but Claudine looked ready to explode. She’d already seemed to have overcome her embarrassment at falsely accusing the coffee vendor.

She turned on her heel and strode back to her stall, luckily far away from Maddie’s truck.

Maddie watched the two reporters talk to the coffee vendor for a few minutes, then they departed.

“I definitely need a health ball.” Maddie popped one into her mouth.

“Me too.” Suzanne followed her example. “Hey, this would be the perfect time to do the Coffee Vision spell, don’t you think?”

"Now?"

"Mrrow!" Trixie seemed to agree with Suzanne.

"Well, I think I do need a coffee after all that." Maddie poured some milk into the jug. "Suzanne?"

Her friend shook her head. "I'm good for now. I had one earlier this morning."

"That's right." Maddie worked the machine, the hissing and burring a comforting sound.

When her latte was ready, she stared at the surface. Clearing her mind, she whispered, "Show me."

The foam swirled, then cleared. Dave Dantzler, the radio personality who had interviewed them earlier, stood in front of the coffee truck.

"That's all?" Maddie whispered in disappointment.

The vision vanished, the latte returning to its normal foamy surface.

"Well?" Suzanne asked impatiently. "Did it show you winning the competition?"

"No." Maddie shook her head. "It only showed Dave Dantzler at the truck."

"Pooh." Suzanne wrinkled her nose.

"Exactly."

A flurry of customers arrived, and Maddie had no time to drink her coffee. After she made the last latte, Suzanne picked up her purse.

"I thought I'd go and get us some food. Do you want to come?"

Tempting as the thought was to explore the rival stalls, Maddie preferred to flop down on the stool next to Trixie and have a break.

"No, I'll stay here."

"Okay. I'll get us something yummy."

"Mrrow!"

"I'll see what I can do, Trix," Suzanne promised.

"Oh, Trixie, you know food for humans isn't good for you – most of it anyway," Maddie reminded the cat. "I brought your dry food with me in case you got hungry."

"Broomf!" Trixie scrunched her face up into what could only be a pout.

"All right," Maddie caved in as she usually did when it came to the feline. "We'll see what Suzanne brings back and if it's suitable for you."

“Mrrow,” Trixie purred, her pouting suddenly forgotten. She nudged Maddie’s hand, demanding to be petted.

As Maddie stroked the Persian, her stomach started to growl. Now that some of the stress of the competition was behind her – apart from waiting to see if she’d won – she realized she hadn’t eaten much all day. She’d been too anxious to eat breakfast, and she’d only nibbled on one health ball so far this morning. She hoped Suzanne found something delicious for lunch.

“How about making me a cappuccino?” Dave Dantzler suddenly appeared at the truck window, startling Maddie.

“Oh – sure.” Maddie got to her feet.

Trixie stared at the man, no longer looking happy and contented.

“On the house, of course.” The man smirked.

“Excuse me?” Maddie frowned.

“It’s the way we do things here.” He wiggled his bushy eyebrows suggestively.

She hesitated. It was only one coffee, and wouldn’t cost her much to give it to him for free, but something about his demand stuck in her throat.

"It's not the way *I* do things," she told him.

"Really?" He affected surprise. "Well, unless you want me to totally disrespect you on air, you'll be giving me complimentary cappuccinos all day." His expression suddenly turned sinister. "You don't want me telling my listeners your coffee is the worst I've ever tasted, do you? I can put you out of business *like that*!"

"My customers know my coffee is good." Maddie straightened her spine. Of all the times Suzanne had to leave the truck!

"Mrrow!" Trixie agreed indignantly, standing on the stool and arching her back, her turquoise eyes fiercely glaring at him.

"And what about having your cat in the truck? Don't you think that's a health code violation?"

"No one has ever said that to me," Maddie said truthfully. "Not even the health inspector."

"Hmm." He rubbed his chin. "Maybe I should put in a call to the inspector *I* know. I bet he'd think differently."

Maddie looked at Trixie. She truly didn't know if the cat had somehow magically enchanted the health inspector who had signed off on their truck, but they'd never had a problem having Trixie with them. Until now.

She'd miss having Trixie at work, and she knew the Persian would feel the same.

"Fine." Maddie slammed the stainless-steel milk jug onto the counter.

"And make it a good one – just like you made in the competition." He had the nerve to wink.

She made the cappuccino as quickly as possible, while still ensuring it was "a good one."

"Here." She slid the paper cup over to him on the counter.

"Thanks." He took a sip, seeming not to realize that she hadn't added her signature art to the cappuccino. There was no way she was going to give him an image of Trixie on the cappuccino – he didn't deserve it.

"I'll be back for another one. Keep them coming like this, and I'll make you sound good on my radio show."

Maddie felt like saying a snarky "Don't bother," but instead just nodded her head, amazed that steam wasn't coming out of her ears. Maybe it was just as well Suzanne wasn't here – she might have had to restrain her friend from jumping over the counter and confronting the guy.

"Brrrr." A low growling sound came behind her. Maddie turned, surprised to see Trixie with an angry look on her face as she glared at the radio personality.

"See you later." He mock-saluted her with his coffee cup before being swallowed up in the crowd.

"It's okay, Trix, he's gone," Maddie soothed the cat. She tentatively stroked the Persian's shoulder, and when Trixie relaxed under the gentle touch, Maddie continued petting her.

"Thank you for being here for me," Maddie murmured. Although Trixie had only been in her life for just over a year, she didn't know what she'd do without her.

"Mrrow," the cat replied softly, nudging her hand.

"As soon as we find out who won the competition, we can go home," she promised her. It was only lunch time but Maddie felt tired already, probably from the excitement of the competition.

"Food!" Suzanne waved a paper bag in the air as she climbed into the van.

The enticing savory smell wafted through the truck.

"What did you get?" Maddie asked, momentarily distracted from her encounter with Dave Dantzler.

"Sliders!" Suzanne pulled out five paper wrapped packages. "Two each for us and one for Trixie."

"Mrrow!" Trixie sniffed the parcels in Maddie's hand.

"Beef, lettuce and tomato. But Trixie's is just beef."

"Thanks." Maddie smiled at her friend. She unwrapped Trixie's treat, crumbling the hot patty into her bowl. "Here you go, Trix. It's hot, though."

Trixie sniffed the pieces of beef, licking at one morsel with her pink tongue, then gobbling it up. Obviously not too hot after all!

Maddie took a bite of the mini-burger, surprised at how hungry she was. After her encounter with the radio personality, she'd thought she'd lost her appetite.

"Good?" Suzanne mumbled, around the burger in her mouth.

"Mm hm." Maddie nodded.

"Mrrow!" Trixie finished the last scrap in her bowl and looked at Maddie expectantly.

"We can share." Maddie gave the cat half of her remaining beef patty.

"I should have bought more." Suzanne sighed as she ate her second slider.

"I'll go." Maybe it would do her good to step outside the truck for a few minutes, and forget all about the horrible radio personality and the way he'd blackmailed her into giving him a free cappuccino.

"Hi!" The short, burly coffee vendor who'd had the altercation with Claudine stepped up to the counter. "I'm Bob. How's it going?"

"Good," Suzanne said with a grin. "I'm Suzanne and this is Maddie."

"And this is Trixie." Maddie introduced the cat.

"Mrrow."

"I meant to introduce myself before the competition but I ran out of time," he said ruefully. His gaze flickered to Trixie and he smiled. "Cute cat."

Trixie seemed to preen at the attention.

"How do you think you went?" Maddie asked, curious.

"Well, the judge seemed to like my cappuccino, but who knows?" He shrugged. "He might be polite to all the contestants, so he doesn't give anything away."

"You could be right." Perhaps he told all the competitors their cappuccino was "charming", Maddie thought.

"Did you add art to the top of the foam?" Suzanne asked.

"Yep. I added a heart," Bob replied.

"That sounds cute," Suzanne replied.

"My customers seem to like it," he said. "I have a café in Redbud Glen, near Aunt Winifred, but I'm thinking of expanding. How's the scene here?"

Suzanne and Maddie looked at each other, their eyes widening.

"I don't think there's room for another coffee shop in Estherville here," Suzanne said. "Maddie and I run our truck here, and there's a café on the other side of the square." She gestured to Claudine's shop. "In fact, the owner, Claudine, entered the competition as well as Maddie."

"Was that the woman who accused me of stealing?" Bob frowned.

"Yep," Suzanne said cheerfully.

He shook his head. "I have no idea what happened. The judging had just finished and she marched up to me and accusing me of stealing her beans. I went over to her stall afterward, and bought a vanilla cappuccino, trying to smooth things over." He shuddered. "She definitely isn't using the same beans I am."

"Yet somehow she still has customers," Maddie pointed out. And it was true. She didn't know why, but there were still people who frequented Claudine's café and she remained in business.

The coffee vendor looked a little disheartened. "Maybe I should stay small a while longer." His eyes gleamed with curiosity. “I’d love to try your coffee, Maddie.”

“Sure. Vanilla cappuccino?”

“Why not?”

As the machine burred and hissed, Suzanne held out the sample plate of health balls. “Try one,” she insisted.

He chewed and swallowed, his eyes widening in appreciation. “These are good.”

Maddie finished making the beverage, adding her signature art to the microfoam. “Here you go.”

“Thanks.” He pulled out his wallet. “What do I owe you?”

“On the house.” Maddie smiled. She didn’t mind making this fellow vendor a free coffee.

“Thanks.” He looked down appreciatively at the image on the foam, and then at Trixie. “That’s a great idea, turning your cat into a work of art.”

“Mrrow!” Trixie agreed.

He took a cautious sip, pleasure creasing his face. And then another.

“Mmm.” He shook his head ruefully. “I think you’re going to win.”

“Really?”

"Yeah. My coffee's good, but it's not quite as good as this. You definitely have talent."

"Thanks." A thrill of satisfaction ran down her spine. Sometimes she thought the only things she was confident about were her coffee making abilities, as well as being able to cast the Coffee Vision spell since she was seven years old. And her friendship with Suzanne – she knew that was totally solid.

"It's a shame there's only one prize," Suzanne said. "Otherwise you might be going to Seattle, too."

"There's always next year – if they decide to run this festival again." He looked around at the buzzing town square. "And by the size of this crowd, it looks like it's already successful."

"Business has been pretty good so far," Maddie said. There had been several lulls in between the wave of customers, but she knew they'd done more business today than they usually did on a Saturday morning.

"Yeah." He nodded. "It was worth closing the shop and coming here – and I couldn't resist entering the competition. Do you know who else entered?"

"Jill, the vendor over there." Maddie gestured to the jolly plump woman's stall. "She's from Aunt Winifred."

"Oh yeah, I've met her. Her coffee is pretty good, too."

"And Claudine. I haven't met the others," Maddie said.

"I think there are a couple of other competitors." He savored the last of his cappuccino. "Well, good luck, Maddie. It was nice meeting you."

"Same here," Maddie said. "And good luck to you, too, Bob."

"Thanks." He smiled, then headed back to his stall, where a couple of customers waited.

"He was nice," Suzanne said. "And so was Jill."

"Yes," Maddie agreed. "If I don't win, I hope either he or Jill does."

"Of course you're going to win," Suzanne declared. "I have total faith in you."

# CHAPTER 4

Finally, mid-afternoon, the time came to announce the winner.

A crowd gathered around the judge's tent. Suzanne squeezed Maddie's hand. Maddie didn't know how the crowd would react to Trixie's presence, or vice versa so, since the day was mild, they'd locked her in the truck, leaving a small window open.

"Thank you for attending the inaugural coffee festival for the Estherville and Aunt Winifred region." The judge cleared his throat. "I know you're all waiting to hear who has won the cappuccino making competition." He waved an envelope in the air, and then opened it. "The winner is … Maddie Goodwell!"

"You won!" Suzanne shrieked, jumping up and down.

Maddie blushed as everyone turned to look at her, but couldn't hide her delight.

"Hmmpf!" Claudine snorted. "There must be some mistake. Mr. Grenville," she called out. "Are you sure that is correct?"

"Yes, Ms. Claxton," the judge said patiently. "Maddie Goodwell made the best cappuccino today."

Claudine glowered at him, turned on her heel, and barged through the crowd back to her stall. Although she had her coffee shop on the far side of the town square, the organizers had wanted all the vendors inside the one space.

"Ms. Goodwell, you will be going on to compete in the barista competition held in Seattle next month," the judge informed her. He reached behind him and presented her with a small gold trophy in the form of a coffee cup. "And here is your prize."

The crowd parted for her as she took the few steps necessary to reach the judge.

"Thank you," she murmured, shaking his hand.

The crowd cheered and applauded. She looked out, her heart suddenly stopping as she spied Suzanne's brother on the edge of the throng, a big smile on his face.

"I knew you'd do it!" Suzanne rushed to hug her as the gathering began to disperse, the other vendors talking about packing up and going home.

"Thanks." Maddie returned the embrace. "We'll have to show Trixie." She held up the trophy to Suzanne.

"She's going to love it," Suzanne grinned.

"Congratulations, dear." Maddie's mother hugged her. "I'm so proud of you."

"Thanks, Mom," Maddie replied.

"Well done," her father said gruffly.

"Make sure you practice a lot for this big competition in Seattle," her mother told her. "You'll be up against stiffer competition than here."

"Yes, Mom." Maddie refrained from rolling her eyes. She knew her mother meant well.

"Why don't you and Suzanne come over for dinner tomorrow night? We haven't seen you in a while."

"Thanks, Mrs. Goodwell," Suzanne spoke up. "That would be great."

"And you can even bring Trixie," her mother added.

"Thanks, Mom." Her mother was a good cook and she was right – it had been a while since Maddie had visited them. She'd been practicing for the competition, and last month she and Suzanne had been busy solving their first – and hopefully last – murder.

After Maddie's parents left, Suzanne's brother greeted them.

"Congrats, Mads," he said, his green eyes twinkling.

"Thanks, Luke," she said breathlessly.

"I thought you were going off with the guys somewhere this afternoon," Suzanne remarked.

He shrugged, crimson staining his cheekbones. "I thought I'd find out if Maddie won or not."

"And she did." Suzanne punched him in the shoulder. "I told you she would."

"Yeah." He nodded. "I can't believe Claudine harassed the judge like that, though."

"Mm," Maddie said, tongue-tied. Why could she never think of anything to say to Luke? Because she had a major-league crush on him, that was why. She was doomed.

Suzanne looked from Maddie to her brother and back again, apparently deciding to rescue her friend.

"I think we should get going," she announced. "Trixie's waiting for us in the truck, and we can't wait to show her the trophy."

"Sure." Luke smiled. "Give her a pat for me."

Maddie nodded, her mouth so dry she knew she couldn't even emit a squeaky yes.

Suzanne towed Maddie back to the truck. When they reached Brewed from the Bean, Maddie finally exhaled.

"Why can't I say anything to him?" she asked Suzanne.

"Because you've got it bad for him," Suzanne replied, her eyes sparkling.

"Yeah," Maddie agreed gloomily.

"Don't worry." Suzanne patted her shoulder. "I'll help you."

Maddie's eyes widened, but before she could wonder aloud if that would be a good idea, Jill, the coffee vendor, rushed toward them.

"Girls, I just heard! Dave Dantzler, the radio host, is dead!"

# CHAPTER 5

"What?" Maddie turned to face the other woman, conscious that Suzanne had mimicked her actions.

"I just found out," Jill burbled. "They discovered him behind the judge's tent clutching his heart – definitely dead!"

"Are you sure?" Suzanne asked.

"Yep." Jill nodded her head. "He didn't seem like a very nice man. What if he annoyed someone so much, they … murdered him?" She looked sideways at Maddie and seemed to hesitate.

"What is it?" Maddie asked slowly.

"It's just … oh heck, you're going to hear it from someone else, if not me." Jill swallowed. "He held one of your to go cups in his hand and had been drinking one of your coffees when he … died."

"No way!" Suzanne exclaimed. "That can't be possible. Maddie's coffee is the best. It's not as if she put poison in his drink."

There was an awkward silence as the three women stared at each other.

"Mrrow!" Trixie called out to them.

Maddie opened the truck door, grateful for her cat's interruption.

"Mrrow!" Trixie looked at Maddie, concern in her eyes, or that's how it seemed to Maddie.

"It's okay, Trixie," she soothed. "Look, I won." She held out the trophy so the Persian could see it, but couldn't avoid her voice sounding flat.

Surely Jill didn't think she was capable of murder?

Trixie put out a paw to touch the gold colored trophy, then looked up at Maddie.

"Mrrow?"

"You know I didn't hurt Dave Dantzler, don't you?"

Trixie looked at Maddie with her turquoise eyes, intelligence gleaming from their depths.

"Mrrow!" The cat seemed sure that Maddie was innocent.

Was Maddie crazy? Was she reading too much into her cat's meows? But she couldn't shake the feeling – the same feeling she'd experienced when she'd first found Trixie just over a year ago –

that the Persian wasn't just an ordinary cat.

If Trixie was her familiar, did she have powers of her own? Could she see into the future, just like Maddie could when she used the Coffee Vision spell? Did the cat have other abilities that only she knew of?

"Maddie Goodwell!" A male voice boomed from outside the truck.

It couldn't be, could it? Maddie and Trixie stared at each other, before Maddie moved to the serving hatch and opened the window.

Detective Edgewater stood outside the truck. A portly man in his sixties, his gray hair was more salt than pepper, and his brown gaze fixed on them intently. He was dressed in plain clothes – a slightly crumpled brown suit with a white shirt and charcoal tie slightly askew at the neck.

Maddie and Suzanne had met him last month, when he investigated the murder of one of their customers.

And right now, he did not look happy.

Jill took one glance at the detective's face, sketched a wave at Suzanne and Maddie, then hurried back to her stall.

"What can I do for you, detective?" Maddie asked calmly trying to mask her unease.

"Jill just told us," Suzanne burst out. "And there's no way either of us killed him!"

"Calm down," Detective Edgewater advised, shaking his head slightly. His gaze flickered to the inside of the truck, where Trixie sat on her stool. "Hello, Trixie."

"Mrrow," the cat replied in a subdued tone.

"Health ball?" Suzanne grabbed the sample plate and held it out to him. Maddie wondered if she was trying to distract him.

He looked at the plate of morsels covered in shredded coconut, and then at Suzanne.

"You wouldn't be trying to bribe me, would you, Suzanne Taylor?"

"Of course not." Suzanne forced a laugh. "I just know how much you like them."

"I'll pass this time," he told her, although he looked a little regretful at his refusal. He pulled an old-fashioned notebook and pencil out of his jacket pocket.

"First of all, who's Jill?"

"She's a coffee vendor and contestant – the woman who just left," Maddie replied, still standing inside the truck and looking at the detective and Suzanne through the serving hatch. "Her stall is over there." Maddie gestured to the opposite side of the square.

The detective jotted something down in his notebook.

"Okay." He looked at both of them. "You may or may not have heard that Dave Dantzler has been found dead. Behind the judge's tent."

"Yes." Suzanne nodded. "Jill just told us."

"Did she?" Detective Edgewater looked thoughtful.

"And that he was holding one of our cardboard cups," Suzanne continued indignantly.

"That's why I'm here." Detective Edgewater sighed. "Unfortunately, that part is true. The cup had Brewed from the Bean printed on it. And he had cappuccino foam dribbling from his mouth."

Maddie and Suzanne stared at each other. Maddie was certain the dismay on her friend's face mirrored her own.

"Maddie just won the award for best cappuccino," Suzanne found her voice. "There's no way her coffee would have killed him."

"I didn't say it did," the detective told her. "There will be a coroner's report, and I have to get all the details I can. Now, why was he drinking one of your cappuccinos?" He addressed the question to Maddie.

"Just because it was our cup doesn't mean it's one of our coffees," Suzanne interrupted. "Maybe he got it topped up from another vendor."

"Then wouldn't they give him their own paper cup?" the detective asked.

"Maybe he was trying to do his bit for the environment," Suzanne replied. "Cut down on waste."

The detective's eyebrow rose, as if he were skeptical of that theory, but made a note in his little book.

"Miss Goodwell?" Detective Edgewater looked up from his notepad. "Do you know why Dave Dantzler was holding one of your cups when he died?"

Maddie bit her lip. She knew she had to confess. But before she could part her mouth, Claudine came rushing up to the detective, her cheeks flushed red.

"She killed him!" Claudine pointed to Maddie. "Because he was blackmailing her! I overheard everything!"

Maddie froze. Was it possible Claudine was telling the truth?

"What are you talking about?" Suzanne glared at Claudine. "Maddie didn't do anything! You're just trying to make trouble."

"I know what I heard," Claudine said stubbornly, glowering first at Suzanne, then at Maddie, then at Detective Edgewater. "Dave Dantzler threatened to tell his listeners how bad Maddie's coffee is, if she didn't give him free drinks all day long." She sniffed. "I don't know why he didn't come to *me*. I would have gladly given him as much coffee as he wanted – for free. And then he could have told his listeners how good my coffee is and what a travesty it was I didn't win the competition."

"How did you overhear this, Miss …?" Detective Edgewater asked, casting a glance first at Maddie and then back at Claudine.

"Claudine Claxton." Claudine watched him write down her name. "I just happened to be passing by Maddie's truck when I overheard Dave Dantzler threatening her."

"You overheard or you were eavesdropping?" Suzanne scowled at Claudine.

Claudine waved a hand in the air as if Suzanne's question was of no concern to her. "You know how it is, detective. One can't help overhearing conversations when one walks by people."

"One can if they linger on purpose." Suzanne put her hands on her hips, attempting to stare down Claudine.

"Ladies, please," Detective Edgewater said firmly.

Maddie noticed that he hadn't called them "girls". Was that because of Claudine who looked to be in her forties?

"Mrrow?" Trixie said softly.

Maddie glanced at the cat, noticing the worried expression on her furry face. She and Trixie were still in the truck.

"It's okay, Trix." She stroked behind the cat's ear. "Detective Edgewater is asking some questions, that's all."

But was it okay? By the looks on Suzanne and Claudine's faces, it looked like they were ready to duke it out any second.

The detective took control of the situation.

"So, Miss Claxton, you were walking past—" he glanced at the signage on the truck, "Brewed from the Bean and you overheard a snippet of conversation between the victim and Miss Goodwell. Is that right?"

"It was more than a snippet," Claudine said triumphantly. "I clearly heard that man tell Maddie that if she didn't give him free cappuccinos all day, he would bad mouth her on his radio show. And," she drew in a breath, "he also threatened to tell the health inspector about—"

"Detective Edgewater," Maddie called out urgently. "I'll tell you exactly what he said to me, if we can do it in private." She flicked a glance toward Claudine.

"In a minute, Miss Goodwell," the detective replied.

"Anything else?" the detective asked Claudine.

Claudine screwed up her face, as if trying to remember anything else to Maddie's detriment, then finally shook her head.

"No." She looked disappointed. "But I'm sure that cat shouldn't be allowed in a food preparation area."

"Broomf!" Trixie narrowed her eyes to little turquoise slits as she stared at Claudine through the serving hatch.

"Exactly, Trix. *Broomf.*" Maddie nodded in agreement.

"Thank you, Miss Claxton." Detective Edgewater wrote something in his notebook, then dismissed her with a polite smile. "Where can I find you if I need to speak with you again?"

"I have the coffee shop over there." Claudine gestured toward the far side of the town square. "I'm open Monday through Saturday."

"Thank you." He made a notation, then nodded.

But instead of taking her cue to leave, Claudine just stood there, intense curiosity on her face.

No way was Maddie going to confess to the detective while her nemesis was in the vicinity!

"Now I'd like to talk to these ladies alone." Detective Edgewater seemed to realize that Claudine wasn't intending on leaving.

"Oh. Very well, detective." Claudine sniffed, then strolled toward her stall, her movements seeming to be deliberately slow.

But the detective waited in silence until she was out of earshot.

"Now, what's all this about the victim blackmailing you?" Detective Edgewater asked, his eyes keen on Maddie's face.

Maddie continued to stroke Trixie, the soft touch of the feline's fur bolstering her inner strength.

"What Claudine said was true." She took a deep breath as she waited for their reaction.

"Why didn't you tell me?" Suzanne burst out.

"I was going to, Suze, but it was embarrassing. It happened when you left the truck to get lunch. And I didn't want you to worry." She also didn't want Suzanne confronting Dave Dantzler and potentially making the situation worse. "I didn't like the fact he tried to blackmail me, but I didn't kill him."

"Tried to blackmail or actually blackmail you?" The detective's gaze never left her face.

"He actually blackmailed me into giving him free coffees for the rest of the day," Maddie confessed.

"Tell me everything he said," Detective Edgewater ordered.

Maddie did so, noticing Suzanne's face grow redder and redder. When she finished, her friend looked like she would explode.

"I can't believe he did that, Mads," Suzanne forced the words out through her clenched teeth.

"I know," Maddie replied. "And I hated giving in to his demand, but what else could I do? It was only for today, and I didn't want us to lose customers over it, although I don't know how many listeners he has – had – to his radio program. And also—" she hesitated, not sure if she should confess the next part with the detective standing there – "I didn't want Trixie unable to come to work with us when she wants to."

"Mrrow!" Trixie said in agreement.

Detective Edgewater's face softened as he looked at the cat. "Having your cat in the truck is a matter for the health inspector, not me," he said. "And if he's already signed off on you, then I don't see how it's any of my business right now."

Maddie, Suzanne, and Trixie exchanged relieved glances.

"Is there anything else you need to tell me?" the detective continued. "When was the last time you saw him?"

"Maybe ten minutes before we left the truck to find out who won," Maddie offered.

"Were you here, Miss Taylor?" the detective asked.

"No." Suzanne looked guilty. "I went to the bathroom."

"I made him another cappuccino then," Maddie put in. "When Suzanne came back, we locked up the truck, and went to the judge's tent to hear who won the competition."

"Along with everyone else," Suzanne added.

"Where was Trixie?" Detective Edgewater asked, humor edging his mouth.

"Mrrow." Trixie replied, sitting up straight on the stool.

"Here in the truck," Maddie replied. "We left a window open for her. I thought it would be better for her to stay here than be out in the crowd with us."

"When was Dave Dantzler killed?" Suzanne asked.

"So far the approximate time of death puts it just before the judge announced the winner," Detective Edgewater replied. "We won't know more until an autopsy is undertaken."

"What … what killed him?" Maddie wasn't sure if she wanted to know the answer. What if it *had* been her cappuccino? Had she somehow tainted the milk or the coffee subconsciously with her limited amount of witchy powers? Was that even possible? It wasn't as if she'd hated the man and wanted him to die, she'd just been annoyed that he'd backed her into a corner like that. Would that be enough to kill someone without meaning to?

"We don't know yet. But it's already been reported to me that he was heard boasting today that he'd just received a clean bill of health from his doctor." the detective replied. "We won't know exactly what killed him until after the autopsy."

"Will you tell us?" Suzanne asked.

"Well … "

"So we'll be able to put our minds at rest and know it wasn't Maddie's cappuccino that killed him," Suzanne added.

Maddie nodded in agreement.

“I’ll see what I can do,” the detective said. “Now, what else can you tell me about the victim?”

“Nothing,” Maddie said slowly. “I met him for the first time today, and so did Suzanne.”

“Yes,” Suzanne agreed. “I’m afraid I didn’t like him.” She looked at the detective, as if regretting that last sentence. “He seemed very cocky and sure of himself. And now we know he didn’t have a problem bullying people for what he wanted. What if he went too far and threatened the wrong person?”

The detective looked up from his notebook. “Have you ever listened to his radio show?”

“No.” Suzanne shook her head.

“No,” Maddie replied. “I don’t listen to the radio much. If I have some spare time, then I’ll watch a TV show – sometimes with Suzanne, or we go to the movies.”

“Sometimes we watch funny video clips online,” Suzanne added. “Even if I did listen to the radio, I’m sure I wouldn’t have listened to his show. There was something about his voice I didn't like when I met him today."

"Mrrow!" Trixie said in agreement.

"Suzanne and Trixie are right." A little shiver ran down Maddie's spine at the thought of the man – now dead. Not that she wished anyone to be murdered – however odious they might be in real life.

"Thank you." Detective Edgewater snapped his notebook shut. "I know where to find you if I have any more questions for you."

"We're not open on Sundays," Maddie said.

"No problem." The detective nodded. "I have your home addresses."

Maddie and Suzanne looked at each other.

Oh.

"I'll leave you to it." The detective glanced around the square. The other vendors were in the middle of packing up. "I have a couple more people to question, then I'll be back at the station for a while. If you think of anything else, you know how to contact me."

"Yes," Maddie replied.

Suzanne nodded.

They watched the detective stride away, then turned to each other.

"What are we going to do, Suze?"

"I know you didn't kill that – that jerk." Suzanne touched Maddie's arm. "And anyone who knows you will realize you didn't kill him."

"But what about Detective Edgewater?" Maddie asked. "It looks like Dave Dantzler died holding the cappuccino I made for him, and now the detective knows he blackmailed me into giving him free coffees for the day. And I'm sure Claudine will be quick to tell anyone she meets that I'm a killer."

"Not if I have anything to do with it." Suzanne's expression and voice were fierce. "As soon as we pack up, I'll go and give her a piece of my mind. She's an idiot if she thinks anyone will believe her."

"But some might," Maddie said in a small voice. "People who don't know me very well."

"Mrrow." Trixie sounded sad.

Maddie straightened her spine. "There's only one thing for it. We'll have to find out if someone killed him."

## CHAPTER 6

"Mrrow!" Trixie stood up on the stool, her ears alert. She cast a glance of what could only be called approval at Maddie.

"Yes!" Suzanne eyes lit up. "After all, we solved Mrs. Hodgeton's murder last month, didn't we? I'm sure we can do it again."

"Detective Edgewater also solved it, remember?" Maddie pointed out.

"Yeah, but at exactly the same time we did," Suzanne replied. "In fact, you got there before he did. Anyway, we know what we're doing now." Suzanne's strawberry-blonde ponytail swung from side to side in her enthusiasm.

"Mrrow!" Trixie agreed.

Maddie wasn't quite so sure, but she knew she had to do something about the situation, even if that meant investigating the death herself – with the help of Suzanne and Trixie.

"Okay." She looked at the inside of the truck and stifled a groan. She and Suzanne had to pack up before they could drive the truck back to her house. Although they were allowed to park it on the square during the day, the town council didn't allow them to leave it there overnight.

"Let's take the truck back to my place first," Maddie suggested.

They tidied everything away, Suzanne looking at the sample plate of health balls with a frown.

"There are still some left." She showed the plate to Maddie.

"Will they keep?" Maddie asked.

Suzanne shook her head. "Want some?"

Usually, Maddie would take a couple but right now she didn't feel like eating.

A man she'd met today might have been murdered – and she was implicated in the crime.

"No." She attempted a smile. "You have them."

Suzanne covered her mouth as she yawned. "It'll save me from cooking dinner tonight."

"Good idea," Maddie replied.

Once everything was packed up, Maddie and Suzanne jumped into the cab, Maddie starting the engine.

Some of the other vendors had already left, although there were still a couple of sheriff's deputies standing around the judge's tent.

Suzanne snapped her fingers. "Maybe the judge did it. Dave was found outside his tent."

"Maybe," Maddie agreed, concentrating on turning the truck out of the square. There were still some festival goers lingering on the green, as well as heading toward their own vehicles, and she needed to be careful.

Once they were out of the congested area, Maddie's shoulders relaxed.

"He seemed nice, though."

"Who?" Suzanne asked. "Oh, the judge."

"Yes." Maddie turned into her driveway. "I better get Trixie inside. She might want to stretch her legs after being in the truck all day."

"Mrrow!" Trixie agreed.

Maddie carried Trixie to the house, the cat's soft fur caressing her hands.

"Wouldn't it be great if you could do a spell that would open the front door for you?" Suzanne joked, as Maddie juggled keys and Trixie. "Do you want me to take her?"

"I think I've got it." Maddie thrust the key into the lock, the door opening easily. She set down Trixie in the hallway, the Persian scampering along the carpet and into the kitchen.

Maddie fed Trixie in the kitchen, giving the cat her favorite beef and gravy in her turquoise bowl.

"Want something to drink?" Maddie asked Suzanne, opening the refrigerator again. "I've got milk, juice, water, and soda."

"I'll have some juice. Thanks." Suzanne reached up and got out two glasses from the cupboard near the fridge.

Maddie sipped at her glass of orange juice. Trixie licked the beefy bits in her bowl as if it was the finest meal she'd ever eaten, and Suzanne flopped down on a pine kitchen chair.

"I don't know if I could drink a cup of coffee again," Maddie admitted.

"I know what you mean." Suzanne looked sympathetic. "But it wasn't your coffee that killed him, Mads. I'm sure of it."

"I only hope Detective Edgewater is." Maddie set down her glass of orange juice. "So, where do we start? Should we make a list of suspects first?"

"Good idea." Suzanne scanned the bare wooden table that matched the chairs. "Got a pen and paper? Or your laptop?"

"Here." Maddie rifled in a kitchen drawer and pulled out a big notepad and a pen. "This should do for now."

"Okay." Suzanne counted on her fingers. "Besides Dave Dantzler—" she paused for a second "—there was Jill, Bob, Claudine, the judge, and the newspaper reporter. Anyone else?"

"You, me, Trixie—" the feline looked up from her bowl at the mention of her name and then continued eating "—and Ramon."

"There's no way Ramon is a suspect!" Suzanne sounded shocked.

"I agree it's unlikely." At her friend's scowl, Maddie amended it to, "Incredibly unlikely. But he was there – for some of the time at least."

"And so were your parents," Suzanne pointed out. Then she sighed. "And my brother – at the judging."

They stared at each other.

"There's no way your brother killed him," Maddie stated.

"No." Suzanne sighed. "I think coming up with the right suspects is going to be harder than we thought."

"Yep," Maddie agreed, feeling gloomy.

After a couple of minutes of silence, only broken by the white and silver kitchen clock tick-tocking on the wall, Maddie said:

"Maybe we should start with the people Dave interviewed when he accompanied the judge on his rounds."

"Good idea." Suzanne's ponytail bobbed as she nodded. "Maybe he scammed some of the other vendors as well."

"It doesn't seem as if he blackmailed Claudine for free coffee, though." Maddie bit her lip, not wanting to be unkind about the older woman – her nemesis – although sometimes it was hard not to be.

"Yeah," Suzanne agreed. "But you heard what she said to Detective Edgewater – she would have gladly given him free cappuccinos. So maybe she killed him because he didn't want her coffee!"

They looked at each other and burst out laughing.

"It feels wrong to laugh." Maddie sobered.

"I know." Suzanne sipped her orange juice. "But it doesn't sound as if he was a nice man."

"So let's write down who he met during the judging round," Maddie suggested, picking up the pen.

"Okay. You – sorry, Mads, but maybe we should write down everyone we knew he interviewed and then delete the people we know are innocent – like you."

"Agreed." Maddie reluctantly wrote down her own name.

"And Jill," Suzanne continued. "And Bob."

"And Claudine." Maddie wrote down the name of her rival.

"Definitely include her," Suzanne agreed. "And the nice older married couple I met when I went to get us lunch. They mentioned they'd been interviewed by Dave and the newspaper reporter – his name was Walt, wasn't it?"

"Yes." Maddie nodded. Then she frowned. "But I didn't meet that older couple."

"They looked like they were in their late fifties," Suzanne informed her. "I literally bumped into them while waiting in line for the beef sliders, and we got talking. They asked if I was taking part in the competition and I said you were, and then they told me about their interviews. They seemed really sweet."

"Where are they from?" Maddie asked.

"Somewhere near Aunt Winifred." Suzanne scrunched up her face, attempting to remember. "It was pretty noisy at that stall, everyone in line talking to each other, and I didn't quite catch the name."

"I'm sure we can find out if we need to." Maddie wrote down the information Suzanne had given her.

"Maybe you could do a spell!" Suzanne's face brightened.

"Maybe," Maddie said doubtfully. "My powers didn't kick in with that full moon last month."

"I know." Suzanne's expression fell. "I was really hoping they would."

"Me too," Maddie replied. She'd been half expectant and half anxious at the thought of receiving her full powers – if indeed there were full witchy powers for her to receive. What if she couldn't control her new abilities? What if every new spell she tried to cast ended in disaster?

But nothing had happened the night of the full moon, or the day afterward. Even when she'd attempted a new spell from *Wytchcraft for the Chosen*, it hadn't worked. Only the Coffee Vision spell she'd mastered when she was seven had.

And she hadn't tried the Tell the Truth spell again. It had come in handy last month during her and Suzanne's investigation into their customer's murder, but what if she couldn't cast it again? Perhaps she was better off not knowing whether she still had the ability to make that enchantment work.

"When is the full moon this month?" Suzanne asked.

Trixie glanced up from her now empty bowl, looking interested.

"In three days' time," Maddie replied.

"Mrrow!" Trixie said, as if she'd known the answer to Suzanne's question all along.

"Maybe you'll come into your full powers then," Suzanne said.

Towards the back of *Wytchcraft for the Chosen*, a crumbling page had stated that a true witch didn't come into her full powers until she turned seven-and-twenty. Maddie's twenty-seventh birthday was last month.

"Maybe," Maddie said noncommittally. Would she ever find out if she really was a witch? Or perhaps she only had a small gift – the ability to cast the Coffee Vision spell and last month, the Tell the Truth spell.

"So how many suspects do we have?" Suzanne asked, peering over at Maddie's list.

“Six. Me, Jill, Bob, Claudine, and the older married couple I haven’t met. I counted them as two people.”

“I think we should include the judge, and Walt the newspaper reporter,” Suzanne said. “They accompanied Dave on the judging round.”

“Good idea.” Maddie wrote down their names.

“So that’s eight,” Suzanne remarked. “Now cross off your name, and we’ll have seven.”

Maddie slashed a line through her name, glad Suzanne believed in her innocence.

“Seven suspects is a lot, though,” she said to her friend.

“Yes, but at least it’s a starting point,” Suzanne replied.

“Mrrow,” Trixie agreed.

They both looked at the white Persian and smiled.

“So what do you think we should do next, Trix?” Maddie asked.

“Mrrow!” Trixie trotted into the living room, then turned around and looked at them, as if expecting them to follow her.

"I think she wants us to look at the spell book," Maddie said.

"Good idea, Trixie," Suzanne called out. Then she stifled a yawn. "Man, I'm tired."

Maddie glanced at the kitchen clock. "Is it eight p.m. already?" Suzanne's yawn was catching. Maddie covered her mouth with her hand. "Do you want to come over tomorrow and we can look through the book then?"

"Mrrow!" Trixie trotted back into the kitchen, seemingly agreeable to Maddie's suggestion.

"Sounds like a plan." Suzanne smiled, then stood. "I'll get going and come back tomorrow morning, after breakfast."

# CHAPTER 7

Suzanne arrived at Maddie's house at 9.30 a.m. the next morning.

As soon as Suzanne entered the house, Trixie scampered into the living room and sat on the sofa next to *Wytchcraft for the Chosen*.

"We're coming, Trixie." Maddie beckoned to Suzanne and they entered the living room.

"I love looking at this book." Suzanne sat on the other side of the book. "May I?" She gestured to the thick old tome.

"Sure," Maddie replied. She and Suzanne had paged though it a lot over the years, marveling at all the different spells in there, but Maddie had never been able to cast any of them, apart from the Coffee Vision spell, and last month, the Tell the Truth spell.

Trixie made room on the sofa for Maddie to sit on the other side of the book, and perched herself on Maddie's lap.

"Wouldn't it be great if there was a spell in here to find the killer?" Suzanne enthused, handling the fly-spotted pages with care.

"Definitely," Maddie agreed, fairly sure there wasn't such a spell in there. Because wouldn't they have discovered it last month, when they'd investigated their customer's death?

Maddie had looked through the book so many times in the last twenty years, she felt certain she knew all the different kinds of spells the book held. But there were so many different enchantments in the tome – what if two pages had stuck together over the years, hiding just the spell she needed to unmask a killer?

But her hopes were dashed as she looked through the pages with Trixie and Suzanne. There was nothing even close to a Find a Killer spell.

"Why don't we grab the list of suspects and put it inside the book and see what happens?" Suzanne suggested when they reached the end, a faint smell of mustiness perfuming the air.

"Why not?" Maddie rose and headed toward the kitchen where she'd left the suspect list. "Here." She waved it in the air as she hurried back to the sofa. "Let's try it."

Before Maddie stuck the list in the book, she looked at Trixie. The cat looked doubtful. Did the Persian know something she and Suzanne didn't?

Suzanne looked at the book expectantly, but nothing happened. The list of names sat on an open page that described a glamour spell.

"Maybe if you close the book?" Suzanne suggested.

"Okay." She gently shut the book.

Nothing happened.

Trixie made a little noise that could only be described as a snort.

"What do you think we should do, Trixie?" Maddie asked gently.

Trixie looked up at Maddie, as if she expected her human to instantly understand what to do.

When Maddie looked back at her with a puzzled frown on her face, Trixie let out a disappointed, "Broomf!"

Maddie glanced back at the book – still nothing.

Yet … Trixie had seemed sure the answer – or part of the answer – to solving the puzzle of Dave Dantzler's death lay inside the book. Otherwise, why would she have run over to it last night, and again this morning, when Suzanne arrived?

Maybe it wasn't as simple as she and Suzanne had first thought. Maybe she had to try another spell first, and maybe that spell would lead them to either the enchantment they needed, or at least point them in the right direction. Perhaps there would be a lot of legwork involved, just like there had been last month, in their first murder investigation.

"Trixie, do you know which spell I should try?" Maddie asked. When Suzanne looked at her questioningly, she replied, "It's worth a shot."

Trixie nudged the book, then Maddie's hand. Maddie obediently turned the page, then another, as Trixie urged her to explore the book again, ancient page by ancient page.

Finally, Trixie said "Mrrow," and sat back on the sofa.

"It's the Tell the Truth spell," Maddie said, her tone disappointed.

"But you know how to do that one," Suzanne said, brightening.

"Yes, but I haven't tried it again since last month," Maddie replied.

"Broomf!" Trixie chided her.

"Obviously Trixie thinks you should attempt it again."

"Mrrow." Trixie nestled in Maddie's lap.

"Yeah." Maddie sighed. "But what if I can't do it again?"

"And what if you can?" Suzanne pointed out. "That spell helped us last time."

"And it's only the second spell I've been able to do," Maddie said gloomily. "What if I can't do any spells except these two – ever?"

"Then that's two more than most other people can do. Like me." Suzanne's mouth edged into a self-deprecating smile.

"You're right." Maddie saw the humor in the situation. "I can't believe I'm complaining about it. Half the time I worry about what would happen if I did have the ability to cast all these spells in the book, and the other half of the time I wonder what's wrong with me that I can't."

Trixie snuggled into Maddie's lap as if attempting to comfort her.

"Thanks, Trix." Maddie gently stroked the feline.

"So Trixie thinks you need to cast Tell the Truth," Suzanne said. She took out the list of suspects from the book and stared at it. "Well, the book hasn't magically changed the list or anything like that."

"It would have been cool if it had," Maddie said.

"Yeah. And don't forget," Suzanne continued, "the next full moon is only two days away now. Maybe you'll get your full powers then, or at least the ability to cast a new spell."

"Mrrow!" Trixie sat up on Maddie's lap, as if Suzanne had just stated something important.

Maddie and Suzanne looked at the cat, then at each other.

"I wonder …" Maddie said slowly.

"Okay, I'm definitely going to be here for that." Suzanne nodded. "Do you think your powers will kick in that night or the following morning?"

They both looked at Trixie for an answer, but she just stared back at them unblinkingly, her turquoise eyes shining.

"I guess we'll just have to wait and see." Maddie peered at the book. "So I'll write these words down—" she turned over the suspect list and wrote down the incantation on the back "—and put it my purse."

"Perfect. And then you'll have them handy when we question each suspect." Suzanne peered at the words. "I know," she forestalled her friend, "you're not allowed to say them out loud apart from the last two words."

Which were Show Me, the same as in the Coffee Vision spell.

"So who should we interrogate first?" Suzanne asked.

"I wouldn't exactly call it an interrogation," Maddie replied. She turned the list over to scan the names of the suspects. "Should we do it in list order or the people who are closest to us in location?"

"Like Claudine." Suzanne nodded her head, her ponytail swinging wildly. "Yeah, I'd like to interrogate *that* woman."

"I know you would," Maddie said wryly.

"Mrrow!" Trixie agreed.

"So why don't we question Claudine first? She's nearby. And then—" Suzanne scanned the list "—we could go to Aunt Winifred on Tuesday to see Jill."

"Good idea." Maddie nodded. "We were going to visit Jill on Tuesday anyway, remember? Before Dave Dantzler was found … dead."

"Yeah." Suzanne's ponytail bobbed. "So it won't look very strange if we go to see her. And Bob, the other coffee vendor, lives near there, doesn't he? We could stop by his place too, and kill two birds with one stone." As soon as the words popped out of her mouth, she looked regretful.

"And don't forget Claudine is getting a massage tomorrow with Ramon," Maddie said. "I think it's at four o'clock."

"That's right." Suzanne snapped her fingers. "So we'll visit her tomorrow morning during one of our quiet times."

"Mrrow," Trixie agreed.

"Do you want to come with us, Trix?" Maddie asked. "I don't know how Claudine will react if you enter her coffee shop with us, though."

Trixie looked as if she were pondering the question. Maddie wondered if the cat remembered the only time she'd been in Claudine's café, as if her sole purpose there was to meet Maddie for the first time.

Trixie scrunched up her face seemingly in regret. "Broomf," she sounded disappointed.

"I think that's the right decision," Maddie said, stroking Trixie's white fur. "I don't want Claudine scaring you in any way. But you can come to work with us in the truck and stay there while we visit Claudine tomorrow."

"Mrrow." Trixie seemed agreeable to the idea.

"You know," Suzanne remarked, "I'm pretty sure I followed all that. I don't blame you, Trixie, for not wanting to enter that horrible woman's café."

Maddie picked up the suspect list. "We'll have to work out when we interview these other people, too." She tapped the piece of paper with her short fingernail. "There's still the judge, the newspaper reporter, and the older married couple you met in line while buying our lunch."

"That's right." Suzanne nodded. "We should be able to find out more about the couple either tomorrow or Tuesday, when we visit Jill and Bob."

Maddie was silent for a moment.

"What?" Suzanne asked.

"There weren't many entrants in the coffee competition," Maddie said at last, "if these are the only suspects we have. What if the competition in the big Seattle contest next month is stiff? Way too stiff for me? What if I make horrible coffee and embarrass myself?"

"You won't," Suzanne said, patting Maddie's arm. "I told you I have faith in you, Mads. Just because there weren't many entrants to beat yesterday doesn't mean you don't deserve to compete in

Seattle. Your coffee is amazing. Besides," Suzanne said, "the organizers of the Seattle competition don't have a problem with the winner of yesterday's coffee festival competing in their big contest. So you shouldn't, either."

"Thanks." Maddie smiled at her friend. Suzanne was right. Sometimes she needed to have more faith in herself.

After a minute, Maddie said, "But do you think yesterday will affect business tomorrow? What if word's gotten out that the radio personality died holding one of our cups – and drinking the cappuccino I made him?"

"Hmm." Suzanne drummed her finger on her lips. "Of course, they're idiots if they think that's true. On the other hand, business might be even better – everyone checking out the coffee vendor who might be implicated in his death." At Maddie's stricken look, she rushed to add, "I shouldn't have put it like that – sorry. But people will probably be curious about it all – if they've heard anything – and maybe we'll get some new customers. Once they've tasted your coffee and no harm's come to them, I bet they'll be back for more."

"I hope so," Maddie replied.

"And as soon as Detective Edgewater tells us you're in the clear officially, we can tell our customers, and I'll bet they'll tell their friends, and business will be back to normal, or even better – which will make it the new normal."

"Mrrow," Trixie agreed.

"Fingers crossed." Maddie tried to smile.

***

That evening, Maddie drove Trixie and Suzanne to Maddie's parents' house.

Maddie fed Trixie before they left, and Trixie behaved perfectly, sitting in the guest armchair in the living room while the adults ate dinner in the dining room. Although Trixie had only visited Maddie's parents a couple of times previously, she seemed to instinctively know that Maddie's mother would be uncomfortable if she wandered around the dining room, or sat on one of the dining room chairs.

Mrs. Goodwell complimented Maddie on Trixie's behavior, before delving into the subject that had apparently been a hot topic in the Goodwell household that day – the sudden death of radio personality Dave Dantzler.

"Of course, I know you two didn't have anything to do with it," Mrs. Goodwell assured Maddie and Suzanne as they dug into their dessert of homemade apple pie. The main course of her mother's special meatloaf wrapped in crispy bacon had been gratefully received by them, as well as by Maddie's dad.

"How did you hear about it?" Maddie asked when she'd swallowed her mouthful.

"It was in the newspaper this morning," her mother told them.

Maddie and Suzanne looked at each other with wide eyes. Neither of them bought a newspaper, reasoning they could always catch up with news on TV or online.

"Oh," Maddie said.

"Don't worry," Mr. Goodwell spoke, looking up from his dessert plate. "I'm sure the sheriff's department will catch the killer."

"Just like they did last month when your customer died," Mrs. Goodwell added. "The report was very tasteful, actually. Just that the poor man died at the coffee festival and the sheriff was investigating."

"Did it say anything else?" Maddie asked, not sure if she wanted to hear the answer.

"Oh." Her mother waved her hand in the air, as if what she was about to say was of no import. "Only that he was holding one of your coffee cups when he died."

Maddie stifled an "Eek!"

"Is that all?" Suzanne asked.

"Yes, dear." Mrs. Goodwell nodded.

"Do you still have the article?" Suzanne persisted.

"Why, yes," Mrs. Goodwell replied. "It's in the kitchen if you'd like to take a look at it later."

"Thanks, Mom. Maybe we should read it."

"Definitely," Suzanne agreed.

After dinner, Maddie and Suzanne headed toward the kitchen. They pored over the newspaper article.

"Look," Suzanne said. "It's written by Walt, the same reporter who accompanied the judge and Dave yesterday and who interviewed us."

"You're right," Maddie replied. "I wish he hadn't mentioned Dave was holding one of our coffee cups, though."

"But at least he didn't include anything else about you – us."

"Like the fact that Detective Edgewater said Dave had cappuccino foam on his lips? That could very well be my cappuccino foam?" Maddie asked gloomily.

"Well – yeah." Suzanne looked downcast for a moment.

"Now that I really am implicated in Dave's death, it makes it even more important we find out who did it." Maddie straightened her shoulders. "If everyone in town reads this article, we mightn't have any customers at all tomorrow."

"And Claudine might have tons." Suzanne grimaced. "*Our* customers. The sooner we start questioning people, the better."

# CHAPTER 8

The next day, Trixie accompanied Maddie and Suzanne to work. To Maddie's relief, their usual morning crowd was there, albeit a bit thinner than usual.

But apparently, joggers weren't fussy who they bought their bottles of water from. Sweaty, panting runners seemed happy to hand over their money for some cold water, as they staggered over the green lawn of the town square to prop themselves up on the counter of Brewed from the Bean.

"It's been good so far," Suzanne said during their first lull. "I know we're down by a few customers, but considering that newspaper article—"

"I know." Maddie sighed.

"But at least it gives us a chance to interrogate Claudine." A dangerous gleam appeared in Suzanne's eyes. "I think we should go over there right *now*."

"Mrrow." Trixie seemed to agree.

Maddie gazed around the truck. Trixie sat up straight on her stool, looking interested in what she and Suzanne were discussing. There were no potential customers outside. Her friend was right – now was probably the perfect time to question their first suspect.

"Okay. Let's do it."

Maddie locked the truck, making sure the window was open for Trixie. "We won't be long, Trix."

The feline stretched out on the stool and yawned, looking like she was getting ready for a snooze.

"Lucky her," Suzanne said with a smile. "Sometimes I wish I could have a nap whenever I wanted to."

"Me too," Maddie replied with feeling. She usually got up at 6.30 a.m. on workdays. Sunday was the only day she got to sleep late. What would it be like to be a cat and relax whenever you felt like it?

"I'll have to make a batch of health balls later," Suzanne remarked as they walked across the town square toward Claudine's coffee shop. "I didn't get up early today and make some before we opened." She looked guilty at her confession.

"No worries." Maddie smiled at her friend. "You know I don't expect you to go above and beyond to make them."

"I know, but—" Suzanne sighed, "—now I'm used to the extra profit they've been giving us."

"Me too," Maddie said ruefully. If this morning's custom set a new precedent for their business, did that mean they'd have to pay themselves a slightly lower wage every week?

Ever since Suzanne had come up with the idea of making health balls last month, they'd been making a respectable profit on them every day. It had also been her idea in the beginning to sell bottled water to early morning joggers. It was amazing how many exercise enthusiasts didn't carry water on them and were happy to pay for it.

They reached Claudine's café and looked at each other.

"Let's go in together." Maddie took a deep breath and pushed open the door.

They walked side by side into the café, noting that it was just under half full. Maddie recognized some of her customers, who looked a little embarrassed at being caught in there. Not many people in Estherville seemed to like Claudine's coffee, so why was she still in business? It was a mystery Maddie had often pondered ever since she'd quit working for the older woman.

"There's Mrs. Jones," Suzanne murmured as they made their way to the counter. "And Mr. Dunbabbin."

"It's a free country," Maddie said mildly, although she was disappointed that two of their regular customers were now patronizing Claudine's café.

Suzanne didn't answer, letting the frown on her face speak for her.

"Maddie and Suzanne." Claudine's whining nasal voice went straight through Maddie's ears and she suppressed a wince.

"Claudine," Suzanne coolly greeted the older woman.

"What can I do for you?" Claudine smirked. "Some coffee?" She gestured to the occupied tables. "You might have to wait a few minutes though – I've got customers to serve!"

"We just wanted to ask you a few questions," Maddie said.

"Oh?" Claudine's gaze sharpened. "Shouldn't you be in jail, Maddie?"

"What are you implying?" Suzanne squared her shoulders.

"What was obvious to the newspaper reporter when he reported the radio personality's *murder*," Claudine returned. "He was found holding one of your coffee cups."

"First of all, we haven't been told it's murder. But if it was, the killer could have staged that part," Suzanne said hotly. "Maybe *you're* the killer, Claudine. You could have dug out one of our coffee cups from the trash and shoved it in his hand right after you did the deed in order to frame Maddie."

Maddie's eyes widened at her friend's accusation. She and Suzanne hadn't discussed how they were going to handle the interview with Claudine, but she hadn't expected Suzanne to accuse the older woman of murder!

"What about the cappuccino foam on Dave Dantzler's lips?" Claudine countered, her hands on her hips. "The detective seemed to think it was yours."

"That's not proven." Maddie found her voice. "Anyone who knows me will realize I couldn't do something like that."

"No?" Claudine gestured to her semi-occupied café. "That's not what these people think. I've got some new customers today. They're obviously scared about what you would put in their coffee."

"Take that back!" Suzanne ordered.

"Did you see anything suspicious around the time the judge announced the winner?" Maddie decided to plow on with her questions and ignore Suzanne and Claudine's antagonism.

"No." Claudine shook her head. "Only you and this one—" she pointed to Suzanne "—right at the front of the crowd, as if you knew you were going to win." The last words were hissed.

"Anyone who's tasted Maddie's coffee knew she had a great chance at winning." Suzanne rolled her eyes, as if to say, "Well, duh."

"So you didn't see anyone loitering around the judge's tent?" Maddie persisted.

"No," Claudine snapped. "I told you, I didn't see anyone besides you two."

"How did your interview go with Dave and the newspaper reporter?" Maddie held her breath as she waited for the older woman to answer. By the scowl on her face, she wasn't sure if Claudine would answer.

"Fine," Claudine bit out.

"But Dave didn't ask you for a free cappuccino, did he?" Suzanne asked.

For a moment it looked like Claudine wouldn't reply.

"No, he didn't," Claudine finally said. "More fool him."

"I think that's all," Maddie said, not wanting the daggers in Claudine's coal black eyes to pierce her.

"I don't want you girls coming in here again unless you want to buy something," Claudine snapped.

"As if we would," Suzanne retorted.

"Let's go, Suze." Maddie tugged on Suzanne's arm, gesturing to the entrance. "Thanks, Claudine."

It cost her to thank the older woman, but after all, Claudine could have refused to answer any of their questions. But was she telling them the truth? She and Suzanne would have to discuss that possibility later.

"Phew!" Suzanne said once they were outside and heading back to the coffee truck. "I don't know what gets into me when I see that woman."

"I do," Maddie said wryly. "But who knows – maybe her massage with Ramon today will make her less grumpy."

"I don't know how I feel about that," Suzanne admitted. "He was really kind to book an appointment with her, but I don't know if I want to think about his hands – his *magic* hands – touching her."

"Magic?" Maddie quirked an eyebrow.

"You know what I mean. Not magic magic – at least I don't think so." Suzanne stared at Maddie, her eyes wide. "Do you think he's—"

"I don't know." Maddie shrugged.

"Can you sense anything when you're around him?" Suzanne asked curiously. "Like he's got witchy abilities the same as you?"

"No." Maddie shook her head. "But I've never sensed that about anyone I've met. And I don't feel like I've got magical abilities. It's hard to describe." She exhaled. "I feel normal except for when I cast the Coffee Vision spell, and when I cast the Tell the Truth spell. When the spell works, I know it deep inside. But otherwise, I feel completely normal – and human."

"Huh." Suzanne looked thoughtful.

By this time, they reached the truck.

"We're back, Trixie." Maddie opened the door and stepped inside. The feline was still stretched out on the stool, lying on her back, her white furry tummy inviting Maddie to reach out and stroke her.

But Maddie knew from experience that Trixie was ticklish there, and the cat didn't really want anyone to touch her – it was as if she played a game with Maddie.

"Mrrow," Trixie greeted them sleepily, slowly blinking her eyes awake.

"You were right not to go with us." Suzanne flopped on the stool next to the cat. "Claudine is such a witch – oops." She covered her mouth. "I shouldn't haven't said that."

"No," Maddie said, amusement in her voice.

But Trixie didn't seem to take the faux pas so well, sitting up and looking disapprovingly at Suzanne.

"Sorry, Trixie," Suzanne said. "And Maddie."

"I know what you meant," Maddie said with a smile. "But I don't think Trixie did."

"Yeah." Suzanne held out her hand to the cat, then slowly petted her, Trixie allowing the caress. "I think we're good though."

"Looks like it," Maddie replied. She opened the serving window and peered out at the town square. "No customers in the vicinity."

"Hopefully we'll get the usual lunchtime crowd." Suzanne pulled out her phone. "Maybe I should make a list and go to the grocery store while it's quiet. I can whip up a batch of health balls and they might be ready for our lunch customers."

"Good idea. And when you come back, we can discuss whether Claudine was telling the truth or not."

"Do you think she was lying?" Suzanne looked up from her phone and frowned.

"It's a possibility. After all, she didn't have to answer our questions. You know how she feels about us."

"And how we feel about her."

"Mrrow!"

"But she said she didn't see anyone around the judging tent – except us," Suzanne said.

"Do you think that's true?" Maddie asked.

"I don't know. But why would she lie?"

"To cast more suspicion on me?" Maddie gnawed her lip. "Or do you think I'm being paranoid?"

"No way." Suzanne shook her head, her ponytail bobbing. "You've got every right to be suspicious of Claudine – and her answers. Don't forget, she told Detective Edgewater that you killed Dave."

"Yeah," Maddie said ruefully.

"Have you got your suspect list?" Suzanne asked.

"Yep." Maddie dug it out of her purse.

"We better write down what she said," Suzanne suggested. "So we don't forget."

"That's a good point." Maddie made a notation on the piece of paper. "Maybe I should type it up on the laptop when I get home tonight – I don't think this is going to be big enough if we write down everyone's answers on it."

"Mrrow," Trixie said approvingly.

Suzanne went to the grocery store to buy ingredients for the health balls, and Maddie took care of the few customers who arrived in the meantime.

When Suzanne came back with a shopping bag bulging with ingredients, she had a grin on her face.

"Maple macadamia. My own recipe."

Maddie's stomach growled as if on cue. "That sounds delicious."

"They will be."

Suzanne set to work, shooing Maddie away when she tried to help. "I've got this."

Since there weren't any more customers to serve, Maddie sat down on the stool next to Trixie. Suzanne hadn't made this combination before and she was curious to see how it would turn out.

She didn't have to wait long. Suzanne blitzed the ingredients in the food processor, rolled them into small balls, and coated them in shredded coconut.

"Ta da!" Suzanne held out the tray to Maddie. Twenty-four morsels sat neatly on the baking sheet. "What do you think?"

"They look great," Maddie said truthfully, her tummy rumbling once more. "When will they be ready to eat?"

"In one hour. I'll put them in the fridge to firm up."

Trixie looked at the tray, her eyes wide, and tentatively put out one paw, as if to touch one of the balls.

"Not for cats, Trix." Suzanne held up the baking sheet so Trixie couldn't reach it. "Sorry."

"Broomf." Trixie put down her paw and pouted.

"I brought your dry food with me, Trixie." Maddie pulled out the bag of food from a cupboard. "Would you like your lunch now?"

"Mrrow," Trixie said grudgingly as if she didn't quite believe that the health balls could be bad for her.

Maddie poured the hard-little pellets - salmon and tuna flavor - into Trixie's bowl, the food making a rattling noise.

"There you go."

Trixie sniffed the bowl, then deigned to eat a few mouthfuls, her teeth audibly crunching the hard little brown pellets.

"Maybe we should have our lunch now," Maddie suggested, looking out through the serving hatch. "Still no customers."

"I am getting hungry, although it's only 11.30." Suzanne checked her watch. "The lunch rush usually doesn't start 'til noon, so the maple macadamia balls will be ready by 12.30. I bet we're going to sell out by this afternoon."

"I hope so," Maddie replied. Suzanne's new recipe would definitely help their bottom line, and she was looking forward to trying one.

They'd both brought sandwiches from home, and they ate them in the truck. Maddie made a mocha for both of them for dessert while they waited to sample the maple macadamia balls.

"So tomorrow," Suzanne said after finishing her coffee, "we'll visit Jill in

Aunt Winifred. And afterward, we can stop in and see Bob, the other coffee vendor."

"Sounds good," Maddie replied. Then a thought struck her. "But we'll have to close the truck for part of the morning – maybe we can get back in time for the lunch rush."

"Yep." Suzanne nodded. "What time do you think Jill's café opens?"

"Is she online?" Maddie gestured to Suzanne's phone lying on the counter.

"Let me see."

A few seconds later, Suzanne showed Maddie the information on the phone screen. "The opening hours say 9.30 'til 5."

"Great." Maddie smiled. "We can get there as soon as she opens, then visit Bob, and get back here by noon."

Before Suzanne could reply, a customer arrived, putting in an order for a large latte.

The lunch period was busy, although they weren't as slammed as they usually were. Still, Maddie was grateful that a lot of their customers hadn't deserted them – yet.

When Suzanne brought out the tray of maple macadamia balls, Maddie's mouth watered.

"I've saved some for us." Suzanne winked.

Which was just as well. Because as Suzanne had predicted, the health balls sold out.

Finally, Maddie got to try the tempting morsels. Suzanne had saved two each for them.

Maddie sank down on a stool after serving the last customer. The square was now deserted, with employees hurrying back to their jobs, and housewives and seniors returning home.

"Yum," she mumbled around a mouthful of macadamia, maple syrup and coconut. "I think these are the best you've made so far."

"I think so, too." Suzanne looked pleased with herself. "At least they've made us a little extra profit today."

"You've got to make more of them," Maddie ordered with a smile. "If we make another batch this afternoon, they'll be ready for lunch tomorrow when we get back from Aunt Winifred."

"Okay." Suzanne nodded. "I'll go back to the grocery store for more ingredients in a sec. I only bought enough to make this one batch, apart from the bottle of maple syrup."

Trixie had snoozed through the lunch rush, but now sat up on her stool, looking interested.

"They would probably make you sick, Trixie," Maddie told the cat gently. Trying to change the subject, she asked the feline, "Do you want to come with us tomorrow when we interview Jill? She runs a café in Aunt Winifred."

"Mrrow!" Trixie nodded her head. Or was Maddie imagining things?

"Don't forget Jill has a dog," Suzanne pointed out, typing another shopping list on her phone.

"What do you think, Trix?" Maddie looked enquiringly at the Persian. "Do you want to meet Jill's dog?"

Trixie seemed to ponder the question, then said, "Mrrow."

"I think that means yes," Maddie told Suzanne.

"Trixie could wear her harness tomorrow," Suzanne suggested as rose from her stool.

Maddie nodded. Although Trixie was very good when she wore the harness, Maddie suspected she didn't like wearing it that much. But it would be practical for tomorrow, in case Jill's dog was too enthusiastic or didn't like cats.

Suzanne looked out through the serving hatch and pouted. "No customers."

"It will give us a chance to make the maple macadamias when you get back," Maddie said. "Do you think we should make double?"

"Even better – a triple batch." Suzanne grinned. "That way there'll be more for us!"

## CHAPTER 9

The next day, Maddie and Suzanne opened Brewed from the Bean at their usual time of 7.30 a.m., served the sweaty, thirsty joggers and the early morning workers they'd managed to retain, then closed up at 8.45am and walked to Maddie's house nearby.

Trixie had stayed home that morning – Maddie thought it would be easier if they picked up Trixie along with her car to make the trip to Aunt Winifred.

"Mrrow," the white Persian greeted them with a muffled meow as Maddie unlocked the front door, her turquoise harness dangling from her mouth.

"Ready for our road trip, Trixie?" Suzanne greeted the cat with a smile.

"Mrrow!" The cat's eyes sparkled with anticipation.

Maddie quickly put the nylon contraption on Trixie, the Persian standing still for her.

"Let's go." Maddie held the leash and smiled as Trixie led the way out of the house, the cat turning back as if to check Maddie and Suzanne were following her.

"Let me know if you don't like the dog when you meet him, and I'll put you back in the car," Maddie said to Trixie.

"Do you think Jill's dog will be at the café?" Suzanne asked as Maddie drove down the street.

"I don't know." Maddie crinkled her brow. "I just remember Jill saying she didn't bring him to the festival as she wasn't sure it was allowed."

"I guess we'll find out when we get there," Suzanne replied with a smile.

The scenery of tall Douglas firs amidst a rural setting made it a pleasant drive. At exactly 9.30 a.m., Maddie pulled up outside Jill's café in Aunt Winifred.

The town seemed to be a little smaller in size than Estherville, and Jill's café was at the end of the main street which was lined with a variety of small shops.

"Cute," Suzanne remarked as they stared out of the window at the café. Hanging baskets of yellow and purple pansies adorned the outside, while inside looked bright and airy.

“I think it suits her,” Maddie said as she got of the car. She reached back in for Trixie, then set the Persian onto the sidewalk. “What do you think, Trix?”

“Mrrow.” Trixie looked around the street and then at the café, her eyes wide, as if everything about the scene interested her.

The black and white Open sign hung in the front door.

“Let’s go.” Suzanne strode to the clear glass door trimmed with mahogany.

Trixie trotted after Suzanne, and Maddie brought up the rear. Suzanne pushed the door open and they stepped inside.

There were plenty of wooden tables and chairs, all of the same mahogany hue. Prints of pretty flowers decorated the white painted walls. It seemed very charming and friendly.

But they were the only customers.

“Hi!” Jill stepped out of the back and bustled to the counter. She wore blue jeans and a violet jumper, along with a friendly smile. “What can I get you folks? Oh! We met on Saturday at the coffee festival. It's Maddie and Suzanne, right?"

"That's right." Maddie gestured to Trixie. "Is it okay for my cat to visit with us if I keep her on the harness?"

Trixie blinked up at Jill, looking sweet and innocent.

"Oh, your cat is adorable." Jill smiled at the feline. "Sure, I don't have a problem with her being in here. Especially since I don't have any customers at the moment."

"How's business?" Suzanne asked curiously.

"It's okay." Jill shrugged. "It could be a bit better but I've just opened and it's Tuesday. My best days are usually Thursday through Saturday, although I took time off for the festival last week. It should pick up at lunch today."

"That's good," Maddie said.

"Would your cat like a bowl of water?" Jill peered over the counter at Trixie.

"Mrrow," Trixie answered.

"Yes, I think so," Maddie replied with a smile. "Thank you."

"No problem." Jill bent down and fetched a stainless-steel bowl, then filled it up from the sink behind her. "Here you go, sweetie." She stepped from around the counter and placed the bowl away from the front door, but close to the counter on the other side of the room.

Trixie led Maddie to the bowl and started lapping the water, her little pink tongue darting in and out of the bowl.

"I'd love to try your coffee," Maddie said.

"Sure." Jill smiled at them.

"Me too," Suzanne put in. "I'm desperate for a latte."

"You two sit down and I'll bring them over." Jill stepped over to the espresso machine.

"We were interested in what you thought about the festival." Maddie exchanged a swift glance with Suzanne.

Jill tsked over the hissing and grinding of the machine.

"It was terrible about Dave Dantzler, wasn't it?" She looked at Maddie, as if remembering what had happened at the end of the festival.

"Yes," Maddie said truthfully.

“Has the sheriff’s department found out how he died?”

“We haven’t heard anything,” Suzanne replied. “Have you?”

“No.” Jill shook her head and busied herself making the lattes.

“What did you think about the other vendors?” Maddie asked. Trixie had finished drinking the water and was staring up at the counter, watching Jill make the coffee.

“They seemed nice.” Jill poured them each a latte as well as one for herself and gestured to the empty tables. “Why don’t we sit over there? These days I grab any opportunity I can to get off my feet, even this early in the morning.”

Maddie nodded, knowing the feeling. Although she was younger than Jill, she was grateful the truck was big enough to boast stools for her, Trixie, and Suzanne to sit on when there was a lull. When she’d worked at Claudine’s coffee shop, she hadn’t had that luxury, and her feet used to ache at the end of the day.

They all settled at a table large enough for four, Trixie sitting on the fourth chair.

"She's so cute." Jill looked admiringly at her. "I'd love her to meet my dog, Boyd. He's outside in the garden."

"You have a garden at the rear?" Maddie asked. She hadn't seen a hint of one when they'd parked out front.

"Yep. I used to have some tables out there for extra customers, but it was too much work, going outside and coming inside all the time. I have an employee who comes to help me on Thursdays to Saturdays, but on the quiet days I'm on my own. So I decided to bring Boyd to work since he gets lonely by himself at home, and now I play with him in the garden during the quiet times."

"How do you know if you have customers if you're out in the back?" Suzanne wore a puzzled frown.

"I had a bell installed. When someone steps inside, it goes off at the back door." Jill sipped her coffee. "I haven't turned it on yet this morning. I was in the kitchen when you came in, and I can usually hear customers enter the shop from there."

Maddie tried her latte. The foam was good – she enjoyed decent foam – and the coffee had a smooth, light taste.

Perhaps a little too light for her liking, but it was a very good latte.

"Mm." Suzanne smiled as she put down her latte glass. "This is yummy."

"Thanks." Jill smiled. "I thought I might have a chance of winning the competition but it wasn't to be." She glanced at Maddie. "I'd love to taste your coffee sometime, though."

"You're welcome at Brewed from the Bean whenever you like," Maddie said sincerely. She hoped Jill wasn't the killer, because she liked the woman.

"I'll take you up on that," Jill replied. "What are your opening hours?"

"Monday to Friday, 7.30 'til 4, and Saturday 7.30 'til lunch time," Suzanne replied. "What about you? We came over today because we thought you might be closed on Mondays."

"You would be right." Jill nodded. "It's just not worth it for me to open Mondays – or Sundays. Everyone around here goes to church Sunday morning, and then goes home for lunch." She chuckled.

"We get the early morning joggers and office workers," Maddie informed her.

"That's one of the reasons we open on Mondays."

"I think we sell more coffee on Monday mornings than any other day of the week," Suzanne said with a laugh. "People seem to hate going to work on Monday the most, and they treat themselves to an extra shot of espresso to get the working week started."

"It looks like you two know what you're doing," Jill said admiringly.

"I hope so," Maddie replied. "We've only had the coffee truck for seven months."

"And business was down a bit yesterday," Suzanne admitted. "I think it's because some people heard about Dave holding one of our cardboard cups in his hand when he was … found."

Now that they were back on the topic of the potential murder, Maddie ventured, "Did you see anything suspicious, Jill? Around the time of his death?"

The older woman looked thoughtful, staring into space.

"The detective thinks it happened just before the judge announced the winner of the coffee making competition," Maddie added.

"No," Jill replied at last. "I did see Bob talk to Dave about thirty minutes before the judge made his announcement about the winner. I went to get a couple of sliders – you know, those mini hamburgers – for a late lunch, and while I waited in line I thought I saw them saying something to each other. But I didn't get a really good look. Maybe it wasn't Bob." She looked a little worried – was she afraid she'd incriminated the other coffee vendor?

"Those sliders were delicious, weren't they?" Suzanne enthused. "We had them for lunch, too. And while I was there, I bumped into this married couple who looked to be in their fifties, but I didn't catch where they were from."

"Oh, I think I know who you mean," Jill replied, her face brightening. "I visited their stall to see how good their coffee was." She looked apologetic for a second. "I meant to come over to you girls too, after the judging round, but then I got busy with customers, and then they announced you'd won and then—"

"We understand," Maddie said hastily. She didn't blame the other woman for not wanting Maddie to make her a cappuccino after Dave had been found dead with one of Brewed from the Bean's cups in his hand.

"Mrrow," Trixie agreed.

"How was their coffee?" Maddie asked curiously.

"Quite good," Jill replied, "although I realized I preferred mine. They're from a small town between Aunt Winifred and Seattle. I can't remember seeing them at the judging, though."

"Hmm," Maddie murmured. She didn't think they were any closer to finding out the truth, apart from the fact that Bob, the coffee vendor, had spoken to Dave Dantzler not long before he was killed.

"Did you try Bob's coffee?" Suzanne asked.

"Yes." Jill blushed. "I thought it was wonderful. In fact, I even asked him what kind of beans he used. I've been thinking maybe I should serve two different kinds – my usual light roast which you're drinking, and a slightly darker roast for people who want a bit more oomph. Maybe it will tempt my customers to come back more often if they have more choice."

"I think that's a good idea," Maddie said. "Have you tried making a batch of health balls yet?"

"Oh, you must," Suzanne exclaimed before the older woman had a chance to answer.

"Not yet," Jill replied ruefully. "I felt so guilty at leaving Boyd alone all day on Saturday that I took him for a long walk on Sunday and played fetch with him. And yesterday, I'm afraid I just relaxed at home, and took Boyd for another long walk."

"I made maple macadamia balls," Suzanne told her. "They're to die for!" Her face fell as she realized what she'd said. "I didn't mean it like that."

"It's okay." Jill chuckled. "I'll try experimenting later today – I should have time this afternoon after the lunch crowd."

"Mrrow?" Trixie enquired, looking first at Maddie and then at Jill.

“I think she’d like to meet your dog,” Maddie said. “If it’s okay with you.”

“Sure thing.” Jill rose from the table. “But I have to warn you, he might become a bit excited. He hasn’t met a fellow animal he doesn’t like immediately.”

They followed Jill through the kitchen and into the rear.

“I’ll just turn the bell on in case I get any customers.” Jill fiddled with a switch inside the back door. “There. All set.”

She opened the gate into the garden. Green lawn surrounded by small shrubs and flowering bushes made it a pleasant spot. A large, black shaggy dog of indeterminate breed galloped to greet them.

“Woof!” His big red tongue lolled out of his mouth in a smile, and his hairy black eyebrows flecked with gray raised enquiringly as he surveyed the newcomers. The dog’s charcoal eyes shone with friendliness.

“This is Boyd,” Jill introduced them. “Boyd, this is Trixie.”

“Mrrow?” Trixie stared up at the dog with wide eyes. He towered over her, then bowed down in front of her, dipping his head in greeting.

Trixie tentatively put out a white furry paw to touch one of his large black ones. Boyd woofed softly, then cantered toward the center of the garden, looking back as if entreating her to play with him.

"Do you want to, Trix?" Maddie asked. "We'll be here watching in case you need us."

"Mrrow!" The cat looked down at the turquoise harness strap against her fur, and then back at Maddie.

"I think she'll be fine." Jill beamed. "Boyd really seems to like her."

"Okay." She wasn't really worried, Maddie told herself. She and Suzanne would be watching the whole time. "There you go." Maddie unclipped the harness and slid it off Trixie.

The cat seemed to smile at Maddie before racing off in pursuit of Boyd.

They watched the two animals playing a game of tag – or at least that's what it seemed like to Maddie. She wasn't sure what the rules were, though. Trixie and Boyd chased each other in a wide circle, then one of them would turn around and run in the opposite direction, leaving the other to follow.

After a few minutes, Maddie fingered the Tell the Truth spell in her purse. Should she use it on Jill? Did she need to? The thought hadn't occurred to her when she'd been asking Jill questions inside the café. Some detective she was.

"I guess we should be going soon." Suzanne looked at her watch, then at the creatures having fun running around in circles.

"Yes – if we want to visit Bob on the way back to Estherville." Maddie didn't want to cut short Trixie's fun, but her friend was right – they needed to leave if they wanted to get back to Brewed from the Bean for the lunch rush – if there was one.

"Bob said he liked dogs." There was a faraway look in Jill's eye. "Although he doesn't have time to care for one right now."

Maddie and Suzanne exchanged a look.

"Maybe you could visit him and take Boyd with you," Suzanne suggested.

"Oh, I don't know." Jill blushed a pretty pink.

"What have you got to lose?" Maddie asked gently, knowing she was a total hypocrite. She couldn't even say hi to Suzanne's brother without becoming tongue-tied.

"He seems like an interesting guy." Jill seemed to waver.

"Maybe you could take him some health balls." There was a twinkle in Suzanne's eyes.

"Good idea." Jill brightened. "I might just do that."

"I really think we should get going, Mads." Suzanne touched her friend's arm.

"Come back anytime," Jill said with a smile. "And make sure you bring Trixie. I think your cat's made a friend for life with Boyd."

There was an adoring look on Boyd's shaggy face as he ran after the Persian.

"We will," Maddie promised, knowing she'd keep her word, as long as Jill wasn't the killer. She sincerely hoped not – what would happen to Boyd if his owner was sent to jail? Perhaps she would be able to adopt the large dog – if Trixie was okay with the idea – or maybe Suzanne could.

Maddie shook her head. She was getting ahead of herself. And she hadn't attempted the Tell the Truth spell. Did that mean she thought Jill was innocent?

"Trixie," Maddie called. The dog and cat continued to run for a few seconds, then Trixie broke the circle and scampered over to Maddie.

"Mrrow?" Her pink tongue darted out of her mouth and her turquoise eyes sparkled with fun.

"We have to go. We're visiting someone else and then we have to get back to the coffee truck for the lunch time customers." Maddie hoped Jill didn't think she was nuts talking to her cat this way.

Trixie looked disappointed for a second, then seemed to understand. She looked over her shoulder at Boyd, who skidded to a halt behind her.

The feline turned around and raised her head up to the large dog. Boyd tilted his head down, so their noses met.

"Oh, they're saying goodbye." Suzanne's tone was hushed.

"You make sure you bring your cat back for another play date." A misty smile appeared on Jill's face. "The coffee will be on me."

"Definitely," Maddie replied. *As long as you're not the killer.*

# CHAPTER 10

They waved goodbye as they left Jill's café. Maddie had offered to pay for their lattes before they got into the car but Jill had refused her offer, telling her that she might come and visit them one day to try Maddie's coffee.

"I think Jill's got a crush on Bob," Suzanne said as Maddie drove down the street.

"Yes," Maddie replied. "I wonder if he feels the same."

"That would be so cute!" Suzanne grinned.

"Mrrow!" Trixie agreed.

Suzanne turned around to face the back seat. "What about you, Trix? Did you like hanging out with Boyd?"

"Mrrow," Trixie said primly, sitting up straight, as if she wasn't sure she wanted to talk about it.

"Maybe she wants to keep it to herself for now," Maddie said, thinking of her own long time crush on Suzanne's brother.

"Okay." Suzanne turned around to face the front again. "So, did you have a chance to cast the Tell the Truth spell on Jill? I didn't see you do anything obvious."

"No." Maddie shook her head. "She seems so nice. I don't want her to be the killer."

"I know what you mean," Suzanne agreed. "I hope business picks up for her."

"Me too," Maddie replied.

They drove in silence for a few minutes.

"You know what this means, don't you, Mads?" Suzanne said.

"What?"

"I think you should cast the truth spell on Bob."

***

Fifteen minutes later they pulled up outside Bob's coffee shop in a small town called Redbud Glen. The redbud trees lining the main street burst with pink flowers.

Dark wood and the faint strains of soft jazz greeted them as they got out of the car.

"Totally different from Jill's place," Suzanne murmured.

A few passersby strolled along the street, lined with small stores, such as a boutique, a hair salon, and a post office.

From the large windows, Maddie could see that the café was half full.

"Maybe he'll be too busy to talk to us," she said doubtfully.

"Of course he won't," Suzanne chided her. "You're the competition winner. Why wouldn't he want to talk to you?"

"Gee, I don't know." Maddie cast her a dark look. "Because I'm trying to find out if he committed a murder?"

"Make sure you cast the Tell the Truth spell," Suzanne urged. "Then you'll know if he's innocent or not."

"Yes, Mom," Maddie replied with a wry look at Suzanne.

"Does Trixie want to come inside with us?" Suzanne asked, pretending to ignore Maddie's glance.

"Do you, Trix?" Maddie asked the feline.

"Mrrow!" Trixie put her paws on the closed car window, as if doing so would make the door magically open for her. For a fleeting second, Maddie expected it to happen – but it didn't.

"Okay." Maddie scooped up the cat and put her gently on the pavement. "But you'll need to keep your harness on."

The trio walked into the café, Maddie appreciating the rich smell of coffee, chocolate, and baked goods.

"How can I help you?" Bob stood at the counter, wearing a red-checked shirt on his burly frame, and jeans. He smiled in a welcoming manner. Recognition flickered across his face when he realized who they were.

"Maddie. And Suzanne. And Trixie." He bent down to say hello to the feline.

"We were just passing," Suzanne said breezily.

"On our way home from visiting Jill," Maddie added.

"Trixie played with Jill's dog Boyd in the garden," Suzanne said.

Bob smiled. "Jill was telling me about her dog at the festival."

"He's big," Maddie informed him. "But he seems good-natured. And Trixie seemed to have fun playing with him."

"Mrrow." Trixie tilted her head to one side and looked up at Bob.

So far, the feline's reaction to the coffee vendor made Maddie wonder if he was innocent.

"I'd love to have a dog," Bob said, "but I don't think I'd have time. I'm here all day, so I'd only have the early mornings or evenings to walk him."

"Jill has a small garden in the back of her shop," Suzanne put in. "Boyd hangs out there during the day and Jill visits him when she's between customers."

"Good thinking." Bob nodded. "Unfortunately, there's no garden here."

"Why don't you visit Jill one day?" Maddie suggested.

When Bob looked at her, she fumbled on, "So you could meet Boyd, and see how she manages with a dog and running a coffee shop. And you could taste her coffee too," she added lamely when he still didn't reply.

What was she trying to do? Become a matchmaker? But Suzanne was right. The thought of Jill and Bob together *was* cute. Maybe they were meant to be together.

"I might just do that," he said thoughtfully. "I've already tasted her coffee, and now I'm thinking of adding a lighter roast to my menu, to give my customers more variety."

"We'd love to taste yours," Suzanne said. "We didn't get time at the festival."

"Sure thing." He smiled at them. "Cappuccino?" His face fell as if he remembered what had happened at the festival. "Or a latte?"

"Latte," Maddie and Suzanne chorused. "Please," Maddie added. The thought of a cappuccino right now – she shuddered inwardly. She hadn't even made herself one at home since Saturday.

They stood at the counter while he set to work with the espresso machine. Luckily, no new customers had entered the shop.

"I can't believe Dave Dantzler was found dead at the festival," Suzanne said chattily, over the sound of the hissing and burring of the machine. Bob's machine was quieter than others, so Suzanne didn't have to raise her voice much.

"Me neither," Bob replied with a grimace.

Maddie fingered the Tell the Truth spell in her purse. Should she use it now? Or wait another few minutes?

With a deep breath, she drew out the piece of paper. She'd memorized the words, but surreptitiously scanned her handwriting to ensure she'd remembered them correctly.

A calmness descended as she focused. She could see the words in her mind. Silently, she uttered them, whispering, "Show me," at the end.

"What was that?" Bob asked, an expression of inquiry on his face.

He must have hearing like a bat!

"Nothing," Maddie mumbled, her cheeks on fire.

"You have a good atmosphere here." Suzanne deflected attention away from Maddie.

"Yes," Maddie forced herself to say. Now she had to ask him some questions about the murder, so she would know if he was innocent – or guilty.

"Thanks." He smiled, then finished pouring their lattes into glasses. "Here you go." He peered over the counter. "Would your cat like a bowl of water?"

"Mrrow!" Trixie replied.

"That would be kind of you," Maddie replied, realizing with a start Trixie might be thirsty after running around the garden with Jill's dog.

Bob set down a bowl of water for Trixie, out of the way of the foot traffic. There was an empty table nearby.

"Have you got a minute?" Suzanne asked, gesturing to the table. "We'd love to sit and chat with you."

He looked around the café, but no customers seemed to need attention.

"Why not?" he sank onto one of the dark wooden chairs that matched the table. "It's not often I get a break."

"How's business?" Maddie asked, wondering how long she had after casting the spell. Did it have a time limit? So far, she hadn't tested how long the spell could work for.

"Pretty good. That's why I was thinking of expanding. But it wouldn't make sense setting up a second location too far away. I'd be stretched too thin and have to hire extra staff for this place." He looked disappointed for a moment. "Maybe I should wait until the perfect opportunity arrives."

"Do you think you've gotten any extra business since the festival?" Suzanne asked, sipping her latte.

Maddie followed her lead. She allowed herself a few seconds to savor the latte – a rich, dark roast that was very enjoyable – then decided to take advantage of the spell. So far, Bob had answered her question with the truth – she knew it deep inside her.

"Not yet," Bob said ruefully. "But hopefully in the next week or so, after people have had a chance to read our interviews in the paper."

"Same here," Maddie said, realizing she hadn't even thought about the interview she'd given to the newspaper reporter since the murder. When would it appear?

"Have you heard anything about the investigation?" Bob cast her a sideways look. Did that mean he'd heard that the radio personality had been found clutching her coffee cup – or even worse

– that it appeared her cappuccino foam had dribbled from his lips?

"No." Maddie shook her head. "I don't know if you've heard or not—"

"Maddie is totally innocent." Suzanne set down her latte glass with a small thunk.

"Good to know." Bob nodded but Maddie wasn't sure if he believed Suzanne or not. And the Tell the Truth spell wasn't helping her at the moment – was it because *she* had to ask the questions to know for sure if he told the truth?

"Jill told us she saw you talking to Dave about thirty minutes before the judge announced the winner of the contest," Maddie said. Would the spell work now?

"Yes," Bob said, a little reluctantly. "I did."

A deep knowing filled Maddie. The spell was working – Bob was telling the truth right now!

"Why was that?" Suzanne asked.

"I wanted to know when my interview would be on his radio show." He shrugged. "But the guy didn't seem very interested now he'd finished his work for the day. He seemed more focused on drinking as much coffee as he could get his hands on."

Maddie and Suzanne exchanged a look.

"Did he ask you for free cappuccinos, too?" Maddie held her breath.

"Yeah," Bob admitted. "Earlier in the day. And I didn't like the way he practically demanded them, either. But I didn't kill him."

Again, a deep knowing filled Maddie. Bob wasn't the killer!

"He must have been a total coffee addict." Suzanne frowned.

"Did you see him talk to anyone else, before … before …" Maddie didn't know if she could finish the sentence.

Bob did it for her. "Before he died? Yeah. I saw him about five minutes later, after I asked him about my radio interview. He was talking to the judge."

"So that would be about twenty-five minutes before Maddie was announced the winner," Suzanne said thoughtfully.

"About that, I guess." Bob looked at their empty latte glasses. "Can I get you two more coffee?"

"No, thanks." Maddie regretfully refused. She didn't want to become like the victim, totally addicted to the stuff. She tried to have no more than three cups per day, and this had been number two.

"I'm good." Suzanne smiled. "But it was delicious."

"Thanks." Bob looked pleased.

Just then, a middle-aged matron walked into the shop and scanned the tables, as if deciding which one to take.

"If you two will excuse me, it looks like I need to get back to work." Bob scraped his chair back on the wooden floor and hurried over to grab a menu.

All this time, Trixie had been suspiciously quiet. Maddie had been aware of her sitting next to her leg, under the table. Now she poked her head out.

"Mrrow?"

"We're finished, Trix. Do you want to go home or back to the truck for the lunch rush?"

"Mrrow." Trixie yawned, her mouth open wide enough for Maddie to see her white teeth, her pink tongue, and all the way down her throat.

"I bet she wants to go home and have a snooze on the sofa." Suzanne covered her own yawn, albeit a lot smaller than the cat's. "I wish I could join her."

"Me too," Maddie agreed. All this detecting was taking it out of her – or was it the after-effect of using the Tell the Truth spell?

They waved goodbye to Bob and stepped outside, the murmurs of, "Oh, look at the cat," reaching their ears as Trixie trotted out of the shop, still wearing her harness.

"Well?" Suzanne demanded once they reached the car. "Did he do it?"

"Shh." Maddie looked around but the street was pretty empty, no eavesdroppers lurking nearby. "No. He's innocent."

"Good." Suzanne looked pleased, then she hesitated. "Are you sure?"

"Yes."

"Well, that's a relief," Suzanne remarked once they were in the car. "Now all we have to do is get Bob and Jill together."

"Providing she's not the killer," Maddie reminded her friend as she started the ignition, the chugging noise of the engine providing a backdrop to their conversation.

She cast a look in the rear-view mirror. Trixie had curled up as well as she could in the back seat, and seemed to be asleep.

"She can't be." Suzanne's lips firmed. "She's too nice. And she has a friendly dog as well. Trixie didn't seem to sense anything up with Jill or her dog."

"No," Maddie agreed, as they turned onto the highway back to Estherville. "But if this is murder, and Jill and Bob didn't kill Dave Dantzler, then who did?"

# CHAPTER 11

Maddie dropped off Trixie at home, settling the sleepy cat onto the sofa, and putting out some dry food in her bowl, as well as refreshing her water.

Then she and Suzanne walked back to the town square, just in time for most of the lunch rush.

Just like the day before, they were busy but not as busy as usual. Did people still think she killed Dave Dantzler, Maddie wondered as she made a cappuccino for one of her regular customers, trying not to shudder as she did so.

Luckily, this particular customer must not have heard about what happened at the coffee festival, or how the radio personality was found, or they might have had second thoughts about ordering that particular beverage.

When their lunchtime customers had drifted away, Suzanne flopped on a stool.

"Hey!" She snapped her fingers. "I wonder how Claudine's massage with Ramon went yesterday afternoon."

"That's something I'd rather not think about," Maddie replied, sinking on the neighboring stool.

"I know what you mean." Her friend's upbeat mood suddenly turned glum. "Ramon's hands on her back, Ramon's sexy voice, Ramon's—"

"Maybe it will make her feel better and she won't be so – so …" Maddie tried to think of something nice to say about her nemesis. After their morning of investigating, thinking about Claudine was more than she wanted to do. It also reminded her of one thing – Claudine had probably enjoyed the best massage of her life, if Suzanne's experience had been anything to go by, whereas Maddie was too timid to book a session with the sexy Spaniard.

"I hope Ramon survived the experience." Suzanne sipped her bottle of water. "Maybe I should go over there later and check on him."

"Maybe you should," Maddie teased her.

"But I'd need an excuse to just stop by," Suzanne said thoughtfully.

"You could book another massage."

"Yeah." A dreamy look crossed Suzanne's face. "But maybe not so soon – oh, I know! I could ask him if he saw anyone acting suspiciously near the judging tent around the time of the murder."

"Good idea." Maddie nodded. After a comfortable silence, she cleared her throat. There were no customers in the vicinity, and this thought had been preying on her mind ever since the murder had occurred.

"Suzanne, do you think your brother Luke thinks I'm guilty?" Her voice was smaller than she'd meant it to be.

"No." Suzanne's ponytail swung fiercely as she shook her head. "No way."

"Are you sure?" Maddie asked, wanting to believe her friend. What would she do if Luke thought she had something to do with the radio personality's death?

"Of course I'm sure." Suzanne nodded so hard, Maddie was surprised her head didn't fall off. "The only reason he hasn't been by the truck is he's been busy working on his clients' cars."

"Thanks." Maddie smiled softly at her friend, glad of her support.

After they first opened the truck, Suzanne's brother rarely stopped by. Maddie assumed it was because he was busy with his classic vehicle restoration business and that he wasn't attracted to her, just thought of her as his little sister's friend. But now, Suzanne's words had her wondering. Would he really visit Brewed from the Bean to tell her he thought she was innocent?

***

On Wednesday morning, after the mid-morning crowd had dispersed, they received a visitor at the truck. Trixie had stayed home that day, sitting next to the spell book on the sofa. Did Trixie know something Maddie didn't? Tonight was the full moon. Did that mean she would get her full powers tonight – or at least the ability to cast different spells?

"Miss Goodwell and Miss Taylor," Detective Edgewater greeted them.

"Oh, hi, Detective Edgewater," Maddie said, surprised to see him. He'd mentioned on Saturday that he'd try to give them the results of the autopsy, but she and Suzanne had been so busy interviewing Jill and Bob yesterday, that a visit from the detective had slipped her mind.

"Detective Edgewater." Suzanne bounced to the window, a plate of health balls in her hands. "These are my new tempters – maple macadamia."

The detective cast a lingering glance at the coconut crusted morsels before snapping his attention back to them.

"Maybe later. Right now I've got some news for you." He observed their worried faces and his tone softened, "Good news. We've got the results of the toxicology report. It wasn't your coffee that killed Dave Dantzler, Miss Goodwell. It was digoxin."

"I told you Maddie didn't do it!" Suzanne grinned, then sobered. "Digoxin. Isn't that something to do with foxgloves?"

"Yep," the detective answered. "And it's also used in heart medication. We're in the process of contacting his primary care doctor right now to see if that type of medication was prescribed to him, even though he was overheard on the day of the coffee festival boasting about his good health."

"If he was taking that kind of medication, does that mean he accidentally took an overdose?" Maddie asked.

"It could," the detective replied. "But if it wasn't prescribed medication, it looks as if his death was murder."

"What about the middle-aged couple at the festival?" Maddie asked, remembering they were on the suspect list, although she hadn't met them, let alone seen them that day.

"They entered the cappuccino making competition," Suzanne added. "I met them when I was getting lunch."

"They've been cleared," the detective told them. "I already contacted them to see where they were at the time of the incident, and they'd just arrived at the hospital to see their daughter give birth. Their daughter went into labor early."

"Oh." Suzanne sound disappointed for a second. "I'm glad they're innocent though – they seemed really nice."

"I don't want you two investigating," Detective Edgewater stated, shaking his head. "Leave it to the professionals."

"Who, us?" Suzanne blinked, looking guileless.

***

After the detective left the truck, regretfully saying he didn't have time to get a coffee or even grab a health ball, Maddie and Suzanne stared at each other.

"Murder," Maddie murmured. "Just like we suspected."

"Yeah." Suzanne nodded. "But at least now everyone will know your coffee didn't kill him."

"True."

"So, what do we do now?" Suzanne asked.

"Come over to my house tonight?" Maddie asked. "It's the full moon and right now—" she pulled out her phone and tapped the screen. A live camera feed of Trixie sitting next to *Wytchcraft for the Chosen* filled the small screen "—I think Trixie is waiting for me to come home."

"I'll be there," Suzanne promised. "It will be so cool if you get your full powers tonight – or maybe they won't kick in until tomorrow morning, after the full moon has passed. What do you think?"

Before Maddie could answer, a low sexy male voice greeted them.

"Hello, Maddie and Suzanne."

"Hi Ramon." Suzanne's face lit up at the sight of him. He looked devilishly handsome in tailored chinos and a long-sleeved midnight blue shirt.

"Hi," Maddie echoed, wondering how any man could be so good looking. But for once, she didn't feel so flustered in his presence. Was it because she'd seen Suzanne's brother on Saturday, and the short amount of time she'd spent in his presence had re-confirmed her longstanding crush on him?

Still, she thought, as her gaze flickered over Ramon, she didn't know if she was brave enough to book a massage with him – yet.

"I was just about to stop by your salon," Suzanne said brightly as she leaned over the serving window, as if to be as close to the sexy European as possible.

"Would you like to book another massage?" Ramon asked, an interested gleam in his eye.

"Oh – um—"

Maddie rarely saw her friend flustered.

"Yes," Suzanne finally said. "How about later this week?"

"Perfect," Ramon said, digging out his phone and consulting his calendar. "Friday at three o'clock?"

Suzanne looked at Maddie, her eyebrows raised in inquiry. Maddie nodded.

"Yes," Suzanne said a little breathlessly.

"Coffee?" Maddie indicated the machine.

"I think I will have an espresso today," Ramon replied with a smile. "I forgot to give you my congratulations for winning the cappuccino competition on Saturday."

"Oh, thanks." Now it was Maddie's turn to be a little flustered. She busied herself with the machine. Ramon was something of a coffee aficionado, and she didn't want to serve him less than her best.

"Now you will have to beat them all in Seattle," Ramon continued.

"She definitely will," Suzanne replied.

"I might not," Maddie protested, pouring the shot into a small paper cup.

"But I think you will have a good chance," Ramon said, his sexy voice serious.

"Thanks." Maddie handed him his espresso as Suzanne took his payment.

"Maple macadamia?" Suzanne held out the plate of health balls. "And since it's you, Ramon, you can have one on the house."

"Mmm." He plucked a morsel from the plate and popped it into his mouth.

"That reminds me," Suzanne sounded innocent. "Did you see anyone lurking near the judge's tent before Maddie was announced as the winner?"

"No." He frowned in concern. "Is it important?"

"Detective Edgewater has just told us that it wasn't Maddie's coffee that killed Dave Dantzler."

"That is good to know," Ramon said gravely. "Not that I thought it was true." Regret flickered across his face. "I meant to come by before today to let you know I thought you were innocent, but I have had so many appointments in the last two days I have not had a minute to do anything else."

"We understand," Maddie said, glad business was good for him. She knew what it was like to be so rushed off her feet that she couldn't think about anything else apart from making the next coffee in the queue. Would business ever be that good again?

"Were you there when the judge made his announcement?" Suzanne persisted.

"Yes, but I was at the back of the crowd," he replied, tasting his espresso. Pleasure creased his handsome features. "This coffee is excellent, Maddie."

"Thanks." She smiled, pleasure fluttering through her. It was even more rewarding that a connoisseur praised her coffee.

"So you didn't see anything happening near the judge's tent?" Suzanne asked.

A frown marred his face as he appeared to think. "No, Suzanne. I regret I did not see anything strange happen. Or anyone by the judging tent. Why?"

"The detective thinks that's when Dave was murdered," Maddie told him.

"Around the time Maddie was announced the winner," Suzanne put in. "By digoxin!"

"Suzanne!" Maddie frowned at her.

"The detective didn't say it was confidential information," her friend replied.

"That's true," Maddie said thoughtfully. Why not? Did that mean the sheriff's department wanted that information to be made public?

"He was killed by digoxin? That is a heart medication, is it not?" Ramon asked.

"Yep."

"Then luckily for me, I do not have a heart condition," Ramon said lightly.

"I don't either." Suzanne ducked her head as she looked up at him through her lashes.

Maddie watched the two of them, a jolt hitting her. She knew Suzanne had seemed to tease about her attraction to the Spaniard, but was it actually real? And did Ramon feel the same way about her friend?

The two of them chatted and joked for a couple of minutes, then Ramon took his leave, telling Suzanne he would see her on Friday for her massage.

"Darn." Suzanne mock-pouted after he left. "I forgot to ask him how his appointment with Claudine went on Monday."

"Maybe you shouldn't find out," Maddie cautioned her.

"Yeah." Suzanne's shoulders slumped for a second, and then she brightened. "But you're right, Mads. Claudine might feel like a new woman now, and will have a total personality transplant. That's how good his massages are."

"Mm," Maddie replied, wondering what it would be like if Suzanne and Ramon became a couple. Or was that too farfetched? He must be at least thirteen years older than her friend, and as Suzanne had said on the day of the coffee festival, maybe he didn't want to break the heart of every woman in the world by marrying. Would that also apply to dating?

***

They closed up the truck that afternoon. Maddie and Suzanne had decided that she would come home with Maddie and spend the night with her and Trixie.

"What's Trixie doing now?" Suzanne asked as they jumped into the truck.

Maddie pulled up the feed on her phone. "Still guarding the spell book." She handed the phone to her friend so she could see.

"She is so cute."

Trixie sat next to the ancient tome, one paw on the old tattered, hardback cover, as if guarding it from anyone who might want to steal it.

"It's as if she knows it's the full moon tonight," Maddie said, putting her phone away.

"Maybe she does." Suzanne grinned.

They drove back to Maddie's house and parked the truck.

"I wonder what will happen tonight?" Suzanne mused as they entered Maddie's house. "Maybe you'll start glowing when the full moon reaches its peak."

Maddie stopped and stared at her.

"Or something like that," Suzanne said, her tone still upbeat.

"I haven't glowed before," Maddie said, as Trixie came running to greet them.

"Not that you know about." Suzanne bent down to stroke the Persian. "Hi, Trix. Did you have a good day?"

"Mrrow," Trixie said importantly, lifting her face first to Maddie, then to Suzanne.

"It's the full moon tonight," Suzanne remarked.

"Mrrow!"

Maddie shook her head at her friend's enthusiasm. Not for the first time, she wondered if Suzanne should have been the witch. But every time she thought that, she knew, deep down, that it would feel like a part of herself would be missing if she no longer had witchy powers, albeit the ability to only cast two spells so far.

Maddie and Suzanne cooked pasta for dinner, after they gave Trixie her own meal of chicken in gravy. Then they flopped onto the sofa to watch some TV. But Maddie couldn't settle. Would something happen to her tonight once the sky darkened and the full moon glowed over her house?

Trixie continued to sit next to *Wytchcraft for the Chosen*, shifting impatiently from time to time. Did the feline know something Maddie didn't?

Finally, the sky darkened. Suzanne pushed the heavy blue curtains aside and stared out of the window.

"I can see the moon," she said in a hushed tone.

Maddie found herself at the window before she realized she'd moved from the sofa.

The heavy, full moon shone down – was it her imagination, or was the golden moonlight shining directly through the living room window?

"Do you feel any different?" Suzanne asked eagerly.

"No." Maddie shook her head. "But I didn't feel any different last month when I was able to cast the Tell the Truth spell for the first time," she reminded Suzanne.

"Oh." Suzanne's face fell.

"Mrrow." Trixie called them over to the sofa.

"What is it, Trix?" Maddie sat on the other side of the spell book.

"Mrrow." Trixie gently patted the ancient cover of the book with her paw.

"Maybe she wants you to look through the book with her," Suzanne murmured. "Maybe it's the right time." She sat next to Maddie on the sofa.

"Okay." Maddie carefully opened the spell book. The cat looked at her with approval.

"Now what?" Suzanne asked.

"I don't know," Maddie replied in a whisper. Somehow, it suddenly seemed wrong to speak in a normal voice. Maybe there was something magical about the moon tonight, after all.

"Mrrow." Even Trixie's tone was softer.

Maddie turned the first page of the book. "Is this what you want me to do, Trix?"

"Mrrow," the cat practically whispered.

Page by page, Maddie looked through the book. She didn't feel any different. None of the spells leaped out at her, silently begging her to try them. She was nearly at the end of the book when she stopped. Somehow, she suddenly knew this was a spell she could cast.

"What is it?" Suzanne murmured.

"This spell." Maddie pointed to the page.

"How to Escape from your Enemy," Suzanne slowly read out.

"Mrrow," Trixie said, looking pleased.

"I don't have any enemies." Maddie paused. "Do I?"

"What about Claudine?" Suzanne continued to talk in a low tone. "And what happens if we find out who the murderer is? What if somehow he captures you and you need to get away from him?"

“Thanks a lot.” Maddie wrinkled her nose. “That is not exactly encouraging me to keep detecting.”

“It says …” Suzanne hesitated. “Maybe you should read it out. You’re the witch, after all.”

“How to escape from your enemy,” Maddie read the title of the spell. The handwriting was in black ink, faded now through the centuries. And the curly parts of the lettering was a little hard to read at times.

“Say these words three times when it is imperative you must flee from a dangerous person,” Maddie continued. She looked at Suzanne and Trixie. “Maybe I shouldn’t say the words now. You two aren’t dangerous or my enemy.”

“Good point,” Suzanne turned to Trixie. “What do you think, Trix?”

“Mrrow.” Trixie stared intently at the open page.

“Maybe I should memorize it or write it down,” Maddie said.

“What else does the spell say?” Suzanne asked. “Besides the actual incantation.”

“That’s it.” Maddie double-checked the writing on the page. “Yes.”

“Mrrow,” Trixie urged.

“Maybe I should write it down now.” Maddie rose, and headed toward the kitchen to grab a piece of paper.

She wrote down the incantation, noting that this spell seemed to work a little differently from the Coffee Vision one and the Tell the Truth enchantment. For the other two, she had to say the words silently and mutter Show Me at the end of the incantation. For this spell, the instructions were to say the words out loud.

“This is so exciting,” Suzanne still spoke in a hushed tone. She crossed to the window and looked out. “Yes, the full moon is still there.”

She sat back down on the sofa and looked at Maddie expectantly.

“What?” Maddie frowned, tucking the piece of paper into her pocket.

“Do you feel any different now?” she asked.

“No. Not since the last time you asked.” Maddie shook her head. “Apart from knowing I could suddenly cast this

Escape from your Enemy spell, I feel exactly the same."

"Maybe we should keep looking through the book and see if there are any other spells you think you can do now," Suzanne said, her eyes alight with interest.

"Okay." Maddie turned the pages of the book, until she reached the end, but nothing else jumped out at her the way the Escape your Enemy spell had.

"Nothing," she said glumly when she closed the book.

"Huh." Suzanne seemed lost in thought.

Maddie thought Trixie looked a little disappointed, too.

"Perhaps I can only cast one new spell per month with each full moon, now I've turned twenty-seven," Maddie finally said. "Last month I was able to cast the Tell the Truth spell for the first time."

"Then why have you been able to do the Coffee Vision spell since you were seven?" Suzanne frowned.

Maddie shrugged. "Maybe it's the easiest spell in the book?"

"Or maybe you could do it because you became a barista!"

"Mrrow!" Trixie seemed to agree with Suzanne.

"But at this rate, it will probably take years before I attain my full powers – that is, if I'm ever supposed to have full powers." Maddie gently tapped the cover of *Wytchcraft for the Chosen.* "There are over a hundred spells in here."

"If there are twelve full moons per year – then it will take you eight years – before you come into your full powers." Suzanne quickly did the math in her head.

"I'll be thirty-five." Maddie wrinkled her nose.

"Yikes!" Suzanne joked. "You'll be an old lady with orthopedic shoes by then!"

"So will you." Maddie mock-punched her friend's arm.

They giggled, then sobered.

"What does the book say about you coming into your full powers?" Suzanne asked. "Maybe we missed something."

Maddie opened the book and turned toward the back, gently touching a crumbling page.

“It says a true witch doesn’t come into her full powers until she turns seven-and-twenty.”

Suzanne peered over her shoulder to read the ancient handwriting. “You’re right. And you turned twenty-seven – or seven and twenty – last month.”

“But maybe it’s like you said then – maybe they counted time a little differently back then, and according to witchy time, maybe I’m still not twenty-seven.”

“Then when will you be?” Suzanne wore a puzzled frown.

“Beats me.”

“Mrrow!” Trixie joined in.

“Right now I don’t know if she’s agreeing with us or knows something we don’t.” Maddie turned to the cat. “Which is it, Trix?”

But Trixie just looked at Maddie, as if expecting the twenty-seven-year-old to know what her “Mrrow!” had just meant.

“I’m beat.” Suzanne stifled a yawn. “All this magic stuff is more tiring than I thought – and I’m not even the witch!”

“You’re right.” Maddie rose from the sofa. “I think we should go to bed.”

"I wonder when you'll get a chance to use the escape from your enemy spell," Suzanne remarked as they walked toward the back of the house, Trixie trotting next to them.

The cat had evidently given up on expecting Maddie to know what she meant by that last "Mrrow!"

"Hopefully never." Maddie suppressed a shiver.

"But if you do get in a tight spot, at least you'll be able to save yourself," Suzanne said.

"True." Maddie's tone was thoughtful.

She'd made up the guest bed for Suzanne earlier that evening. Now, they stood in the doorway of the tiny guest room.

"You know where everything is," Maddie told her friend as she bid her goodnight.

"Yep." Suzanne smiled. "Thanks for tonight. It's been fun. But I'm sorry the magic stuff didn't quite meet our expectations."

"At least I didn't glow!" Maddie's lips tilted upwards as she and Trixie headed to their own bedroom next door.

# CHAPTER 12

The next day, after the morning rush at Brewed from the Bean, which was almost as busy as normal – yay! – Maddie and Suzanne discussed their plans for the afternoon. Trixie dozed on her stool.

"I think we should interview the judge and the newspaper reporter," Suzanne said. "Don't forget, I'm seeing Ramon tomorrow afternoon."

"As if I could," Maddie teased her friend. Ever since she'd made her booking with Ramon yesterday, Suzanne had worn a dreamy expression when she thought nobody was looking.

"We could go after the lunch rush," Suzanne continued. "And when we get back, I'll make some more health balls."

"Are we out already?" Maddie frowned.

"Yep." Suzanne looked pleased. "They're really helping us maintain our income this week, due to the drop off in coffee customers." She lowered her voice and looked out of the serving window, although there wasn't anyone in the vicinity. "Although now word is out it wasn't your coffee that killed Dave, that might explain why some of our regulars have come back this morning."

"You're right." It had been good to steadily make coffee after coffee this morning, Suzanne giving her the orders and taking the payments. Just like old times – before the coffee festival.

"I'll make a double batch – maple macadamia and the original ones I made – the datey cacao ones."

"You really should give those a name," Maddie said.

"I've been thinking about it, but it hasn't been easy," Suzanne replied. "I mean, datey cacao just doesn't have the same ring as maple macadamia."

"What about cacao coconut?" Maddie suggested.

"You're a genius! That's perfect!"

Maddie smiled, pleased at her friend's enthusiasm.

"Hi." An attractive male voice caught Maddie's attention.

She turned, already blushing. She knew it was Suzanne's brother Luke.

"Hi Luke," she said, ducking her head.

"What are you doing here?" Suzanne stuck her head out of the serving window.

"Thought I'd come by and ask Maddie to make me a latte." He smiled.

"Sure, Luke." Maddie busied herself at the machine, telling herself to ignore the butterflies in her stomach.

"I'm sorry I haven't stopped by before, Maddie." The seriousness in his tone forced her to look up from the machine.

Concern and sincerity crossed his face as he continued speaking. "I know you didn't kill that guy at the coffee festival."

"Thanks," she replied softly.

"We all know she didn't kill him," Suzanne told him. "I just can't believe it's taken you so long to tell her that."

"Sorry." He looked abashed for a second. "I've been swamped with work. And this is the first chance I've had to drop by since the festival."

Since Luke hardly ever stopped by the coffee truck, Maddie was touched that he'd made a special effort to do so.

"All right," Suzanne said finally, as if she accepted his apology, even though it had been for Maddie. "That will be three dollars ninety."

"I can't believe you're charging me. I'm your brother." But he said it good humoredly, digging out his wallet and handing her the money.

"A girl has to make a living." Suzanne gestured to the truck. "And in this case, it's two girls and a cat."

"Hi, Trixie." His eyes crinkled at the corners as he smiled at the feline who'd just woken up. "Are you keeping these two out of trouble?"

"Mrrow," Trixie said playfully, looking up at him with big turquoise eyes.

"We can get into as much trouble as we want," Suzanne informed him, giving him his change.

"As long as I'm around to bail you out, right?" He grinned.

"Exactly." Suzanne's ponytail bobbed as she nodded.

"Thanks for the latte, Maddie." He took a sip, pleasure creasing his face.

"You make the best coffee I've ever tasted."

"You're welcome," she murmured, hoping her cheeks weren't bursting into flames.

After he left the truck, Suzanne turned to Maddie. "I'm *so* getting you two together. You would make such a cute couple!"

"I don't know, Suzanne," Maddie replied. Although she was pleased her friend didn't have any objection to the possibility of her best friend dating her brother, it didn't seem obvious that Luke was attracted to her. "I don't think he sees me that way." Disappointment flickered through her.

"Maybe he doesn't realize it yet," Suzanne said. "I know he's not seeing anyone at the moment."

"He isn't?"

"Nope," Suzanne said with a satisfied smile. "Ooh, I know, you could ask him to help you practice for the competition in Seattle. Someone's got to taste the coffee you make, right? So why not him? He's already in love with your lattes – he just needs to realize it's not just your coffee he likes."

"It is an idea," Maddie said slowly.

"Mrrow!" Trixie sat up straight on her chair.

"See? Trixie agrees with me." Suzanne smiled.

"Okay," Maddie capitulated. Perhaps Suzanne was right. And it would be good for her – because she would be nervous around Luke, and she'd be anxious at the competition next month. Making a good cup of coffee while feeling that way would be something she would need to master if she had any hope of doing well in the Seattle contest.

She'd felt edgy at the coffee festival last weekend, but she knew she'd feel a lot worse in Seattle, with tougher competition, more crowds, and more judges.

"Leave it to me. I'll arrange everything." Suzanne looked gleeful. "Right after we catch the murderer."

"Which murderer?" Claudine's shrill nasal tone made Maddie wince. "Maddie or someone else?" she chuckled at her joke – a harsh, grating sound.

"What are you doing here, Claudine?" Suzanne asked coolly.

Claudine smirked. "Just checking out the competition – and seeing if Maddie's been hauled in for questioning yet."

"Haven't you heard?" Maddie drew herself up to her full height of five foot five. "My coffee did not kill Dave Dantzler."

"What?" Disappointment flashed across Claudine's face for an instant before she masked it.

"That's right," Suzanne chimed in. "Detective Edgewater visited us yesterday to tell us the good news – not that we didn't know already. I told you, Maddie's totally innocent."

"Then what did kill him?" Claudine scowled.

"I don't know if we should tell you," Suzanne said coyly. "The detective didn't say we could go around telling everyone what he said."

Claudine sniffed. "So don't tell me then. I'll find out somehow." She peered at the counter. "What, no health balls? I knew they wouldn't sell." She looked pleased at the thought.

Suzanne tsked. “You shouldn’t make assumptions, Claudine. The reason we don’t have any is that they sold out as soon as I made them.”

Maddie thought that might be a slight exaggeration, but she didn’t blame Suzanne. She was sure Claudine would try the patience of her fairy godmother – that is, if they actually existed. Did they? Maybe fairy godmothers were real, just like magic.

“Humph.” Claudine made a snorting noise. “Whatever.” She stalked off, back to her café on the other side of the town square.

“Wow.” Suzanne whistled. “Ramon’s massage certainly didn’t give her a personality transplant.”

“I know.” Maddie sank on the stool. “I wonder why she comes over here all the time. Is it just to stir up trouble? It’s definitely not to buy a latte.”

“I think she’s jealous of you, Mads. You – we – have it all. Well, apart from me not being a witch or a genius barista. But we’re younger, nicer, prettier – yeah, I know I shouldn’t say that, but it’s true – and we’re running our own business at the age of twenty-seven and doing well overall. We certainly have more customers than she has."

"True," Maddie said thoughtfully. "It's a shame, though, that it looks like Ramon's massage hasn't made her any happier."

"Yeah." Suzanne took a sip from her water bottle. "But maybe Ramon's dodged a bullet there – if it means she doesn't go back to him for more."

"You just want him all for yourself," Maddie teased.

"Yep." Suzanne grinned. "I sure do."

***

That afternoon, after the lunch rush, they locked up the truck and headed to the newspaper office, a block away from the town square. Maddie had left Trixie at home, as she didn't know how the employees would react to a cat visiting them.

"We've got a good excuse to visit Walt, the newspaper reporter," Suzanne said as they neared the one-story tan brick building. “We can ask him when your interview will appear in the paper.”

“And why he mentioned in his article last Sunday that Dave was holding one of our coffee cups when he died,” Maddie said grimly, still smarting at being implicated like that.

“Yeah.” Suzanne snapped her fingers. “That’s an even better reason to stop by his office.”

They pushed open the glass door to the office and walked inside. A receptionist with big dangly earrings and a pink streak in her brown hair greeted them.

“How can I help you?” The girl smiled at them.

From the waiting area, furnished with a couple of chairs, they could see into an open plan office.

The clacking of an unseen keyboard reached their ears, and Maddie caught a glimpse of an older man in a long-sleeved shirt and pants, a pencil behind his ear, rifling through a filing cabinet on the far side of the office.

“We were hoping to talk to Walt,” Suzanne said.

"Yeah, he's in." The receptionist pressed a button the phone. "Walt, there are two people here to see you." She put down the receiver. "Take a seat. He won't be long."

"Thanks." Maddie tried to catch another glimpse of the office beyond the receptionist desk but didn't want to appear nosy. Suzanne, however, didn't have a problem with that – she craned her neck and stood on tiptoes, her gaze scanning the open office.

"I can't see him," Suzanne whispered to Maddie as she sat next to her in the waiting area.

"He must be here somewhere." As soon as Maddie uttered those words, a man stood in front of them, his horn-rimmed spectacles looking a little smudged.

"Hi." He smiled, looking at them curiously. "Maddie and Suzanne, right?"

"Right," Maddie said.

"We were wondering when the interview you did with Maddie would be in the newspaper," Suzanne blurted out.

"Come with me." He beckoned to them, and they stood, following him.

Walt stopped by a wooden desk covered with papers and a large monitor.

"Here." He dragged a couple of chairs from nearby empty desks, and offered them to Maddie and Suzanne.

"How's business?" Suzanne asked as she looked at the office, half the desks vacant.

"Not as good as it used to be." He looked rueful. "But the paper's still chugging along."

"That's good," Maddie replied, noticing a photo on his desk. Against an ocean background edged with palm trees, Walt stood next to an older lady who looked to be in her seventies, his arm around her shoulders. They both wore floral Hawaiian shirts and smiled into the camera, the woman's silver bracelet glinting in the sunlight.

"My mother." He noticed Maddie's glance and gestured at the photo. "She's a widow. I help her as much as I can."

"Oh," Maddie's voice was soft. She didn't know what else to say.

"So what can I do for you two?" Walt cleared his throat.

"We wanted to know when Maddie's interview will be in the paper," Suzanne began, "and also why you mentioned in your article in the Sunday newspaper that Dave Dantzler held one of our coffee cups in his hand."

"That's because he did." Walt frowned. "I have a responsibility to report the news. This paper tries to cover everything that happens in the area, and Dave being found dead at the coffee festival was front-page news. My editor approved it."

"Is that him?" Suzanne motioned to the older man they'd seen earlier – the one with the pencil stuck behind his ear.

"Yeah, that's Arthur," Walt replied. "And if you read the article, you'll notice I didn't mention that Dave had cappuccino foam dribbling from his lips that could have been from one of Maddie's cappuccinos."

"But it wasn't," Maddie felt compelled to inform him. "And … thanks for not mentioning that bit in the paper."

"Maddie's been cleared by Detective Edgewater," Suzanne told him. "It wasn't her coffee that killed him."

"Glad to hear it." Walt gave them a small smile. He pressed a few buttons on the keyboard and a calendar appeared on the monitor. "As for your article, it should be in tomorrow's paper. It would have appeared sooner, but my editor wanted to run with Dave's death which is why the festival interviews were bumped."

"Thanks," Maddie replied.

"Do you know if the sheriff has a suspect yet?" Suzanne asked.

"Nope." He looked at her with interest. "Why? Do you know something?"

"No," Suzanne said regretfully. "But since Detective Edgewater had to consider Maddie a suspect until she was ruled out, we've taken an interest in the case. We were told an overdose of digoxin killed Dave."

"Suzanne!" Maddie hissed. She didn't know if they were allowed to disclose that information to anyone or not.

"Yeah, I heard about that," Walt replied.

"How?" Suzanne asked eagerly.

He tapped his nose. "I have my sources."

Would now be a good time to try the Tell the Truth spell on Walt? Suzanne looked as if she was about to ask him another question.

By now, Maddie knew the words by heart. Still, her fingers found the piece of paper in her purse, and kept in contact with it as she silently recited the words. "Show me," she whispered, hoping Walt wouldn't hear her.

"Did you see anyone by the judging tent just before I was announced as the winner?" Maddie asked.

"No." He shook his head. "But, there was a scandal about the judge, Edward Grenville, a while ago."

"Really?" Suzanne leaned in.

"Dave interviewed him on his show – I think it was last year," Walt told them. "He accused the judge of taking bribes at other coffee making competitions, including one of the big Seattle competitions – like the one you're going to compete in next month, Maddie." Walt glanced at her.

Maddie had listened intently to Walt, but didn't feel anything at all. Not the deep-down certainty that he was telling the truth in answer to her question. She frowned. Did that mean the spell wasn't working?

"What?" Suzanne stared at the reporter.

"Yep." He nodded. "It did major damage to the judge's reputation." He chuckled mirthlessly. "And the allegations were untrue. There had been accusations about this judge, Grenville, which turned out to be total fabrications, and it had all gone down before Dave interviewed him on his show. He was just raking up an old scandal, and didn't allow Grenville to correct him. Just cut him off when he tried." Walt shrugged. "So although I didn't see anyone near the judging tent at the time of the murder, I would say the judge had a good reason to want Dave dead."

"How do you know all this?" Maddie asked.

"The judge came to us after the radio show last year and asked us to print the truth," he replied. "Which we did. But by that time the damage was done. Why do you think a judge of Edward Grenville's caliber was at the coffee festival? It might have been good business for Estherville, but it's not in the same league as the big Seattle competition next month."

Maddie nodded, wondering once again if she would be out of her depth in Seattle.

But she still didn't know if Walt was telling the truth or not. Did that mean she was now unable to cast this particular spell? Or maybe – maybe she wasn't a witch at all. Maybe the full moon last night had taken away her powers to do spells.

But if that was true, then why had she been compelled to write down the Escape your Enemy spell? That was the only spell in *Wytchcraft for the Chosen* last night that had leaped out at her. Would she be able to cast that new spell? Maddie hoped she'd never be in the unfortunate situation to find out!

Suzanne looked at Maddie, as if expecting her to ask another question. But how could she, when she was unsure if the Tell the Truth spell was even working?

"Well … thanks," Maddie finally said, shooting Suzanne a defeated look.

"Um … yeah." Suzanne rose. "We'll definitely buy the newspaper tomorrow and check out Maddie's interview."

"You won't be disappointed." Walt smiled.

As soon as they left the office, Suzanne stopped in the middle of the sidewalk and turned to Maddie.

"What happened in there?"

Maddie looked around but there were only a couple of people on the opposite side of the street. Still, she didn't want to take any chances.

"Not here," she murmured, striding to the town square. "I'll tell you when we're inside the truck."

A few minutes later they were inside Brewed from the Bean. Luckily – or unluckily – there weren't any customers waiting for them to reopen. Maddie made sure the serving window was locked before she spoke.

"I don't think the Tell the Truth spell worked."

"What?" Suzanne stared at her with wide eyes.

"I didn't feel anything." Maddie shrugged in frustration. "I couldn't discern whether he was telling the truth or lying."

"Maybe he *was* lying," Suzanne suggested. "The other two people you've tried it on turned out to be telling the truth and you said that somehow deep down you could tell."

"Yeah," Maddie said glumly. "But today I didn't get that feeling of certainty. And if he was lying, wouldn't I also get the same kind of feeling?"

"You're the witch, not me." Suzanne's face was a mask of disappointment.

"Not much of one." Maddie's shoulders slumped.

Suzanne patted her on the back. "You're learning, that's all. Maybe the full moon last night made things go a bit wonky."

"That's one way of describing it."

"Hey!" Suzanne snapped her fingers. "Maybe there's something in the book about this spell that we've missed."

"Like what?"

"I don't know." Suzanne shrugged. "Something about the way you have to cast it – are you sure you did it right?"

"I cast it the same way I did on Tuesday at Bob's coffee shop."

"Oh." Suzanne's brow was furrowed in thought. "Perhaps there's something we missed in the book about the full moon," she eventually suggested. "Or this particular spell. We should go back to your place right now and find out!"

Maddie looked at her watch. "It's three o'clock. We don't usually close until four."

Suzanne unlocked the serving hatch and peeked out at the town square.

"And there isn't anyone here demanding a cup of coffee either. So now is the perfect time to get some witchy stuff done."

"What about the health balls?" Maddie pointed out. "I thought you wanted to make some more this afternoon."

"Darn. I guess we could buy the ingredients on the way back to your house, then ask Trixie to show us the info in the book we've missed about either the Tell the Truth spell or the full moon. Or both!"

"You think Trixie will know?" Maddie asked.

“I think she knows more than us,” Suzanne said.

“True.” Maddie nodded. “I just wish she could speak English sometimes. Then we would know everything she knows or senses about the book.”

“Maybe there’s a spell in there about that.” Suzanne’s eyes lit up. “Or one that can make you understand cat!”

# CHAPTER 13

They went to the small grocery store just off the town square to stock up on ingredients for the health balls, then drove the truck back to Maddie's house. Maddie felt a little guilty for closing up early, but Suzanne had been right – there weren't any customers.

"Tell me again why we're still investigating now that I've – we've – been cleared," Maddie said as she pulled up outside her house.

"We still haven't got all our customers back," Suzanne replied, as if their customers were missing sheep that needed to be rounded up and brought back to them. "So maybe all of them haven't heard yet that you're – we're – totally innocent. If we can help Detective Edgewater catch the murderer, we can ask Walt to write a story about our involvement and *how we were totally innocent in the first place.* Word will get out, and our missing regulars will come back, feeling guilty that they doubted us in the first place, and maybe even buy extra large drinks or more health balls to try and make it up to us in a customer sort of way."

"That makes sense … I guess." Maddie knew it did in Suzanne logic.

"I wonder if your radio interview will still go ahead?" Suzanne mused as they walked up to the house. "Will they get a replacement host for the show? Or will they axe it?"

"That's a good idea," Maddie said as she opened the front door. Trixie scampered down the hall to greet them. "Maybe this has nothing to do with coffee at all. Maybe it's got to do with the radio station. With Dave out of the way, who would benefit from his death?"

Maddie and Suzanne stared at each other as they realized they might have been looking at things all wrong.

***

Suzanne was a hotbed of impatience at the thought that perhaps someone at the radio station was the killer.

"But we still haven't spoken to the judge," Maddie reasoned with her. "Or checked *Wytchcraft for the Chosen* to find out why the Tell the Truth spell didn't work this afternoon."

"You're right." Suzanne shot her a rueful smile. "But what if the murderer really is someone from the radio station?"

"Do you think Detective Edgewater is covering that angle?" Maddie asked.

"Probably." Suzanne looked downcast for a second.

"Catching killers is what he's paid to do," Maddie pointed out. By this stage they were in the living room, sitting on the smoky blue sofa with Trixie and *Wytchcraft for the Chosen.*

"Yes, but don't forget we also discovered who murdered Joan, our customer, last month," Suzanne said, her ponytail bobbing.

"Mrrow." Trixie delicately placed a paw on the ancient tome. She sat on Maddie's lap, while Suzanne sat on the other side of the magical book.

"Okay, Trix." Maddie stroked the cat. "We'll look at the book now."

"Good idea." Suzanne smiled at Maddie and the feline. "Why didn't the Tell the Truth spell work, Trixie?"

Trixie blinked at Suzanne, then stared at the book. Maddie opened the front cover of *Wytchcraft for the Chosen*, carefully paging through the crumbling book.

"Maybe we should look at the page the truth spell is on," she suggested as she finally reached that section. None of the other spells had tugged at her as she'd glanced at them.

"How to discover if someone is telling the truth," she read out.

Trixie's ears pricked up. Maddie scanned the page, but couldn't find anything that explained why she hadn't been able to make the spell work that day.

"I can't see anything different on this page." She pushed the book over to Suzanne.

Suzanne studied the page, eventually giving it back to Maddie and Trixie. "Me neither."

"Mrrow!" Trixie's paw hovered over the bottom of the page, where it was blank.

"What is it, Trix?" Maddie frowned. "There's no writing here."

"Mrrow." Trixie frowned up at Maddie, as if she was missing something obvious.

"Can you sense anything?" Suzanne asked.

"No." Maddie crinkled her brow. "Nothing feels different to me."

"Obviously Trixie thinks there's something there that we've missed."

"Mrrow." Trixie looked at Suzanne approvingly.

"Mmm." Maddie slowly read through every word of the spell again. There was no addendum, no special instructions anywhere on the page. So why was her cat insisting there was something there?

Unless …

"Invisible ink."

"What?" Suzanne raised her eyebrows.

"Maybe there's invisible ink here." Maddie touched the blank part of the page.

"Ooh!" Suzanne jumped up. "Awesome! So what do we do to make it visible? Is there a spell in there you can do?"

"I don't think so." Maddie cast her mind back, trying to remember every spell in the book. Since she'd gone through the book hundreds of times since she was seven, she had a pretty good idea of what was in there, but sometimes she'd notice a spell that she didn't remember.

"Let's do an online search!" Suzanne dug her phone out of her purse and tapped some buttons. "It says to use an incandescent bulb to reveal the writing. Or a hot stove."

"Maybe trying a light bulb would be safer." Maddie rose, picking up the book. "Come on. We can try my bedside lamp."

They trooped down the hall to Maddie's bedroom. She turned on the small lavender colored lamp – luckily she had an old-fashioned light bulb in it - then held up the book.

"Suze, can you hold the other side of the book?" The book was old – and heavy.

"Sure."

The lightbulb shone on the page, revealing spidery white writing on the fly-spotted page.

"It's working!" Suzanne was in danger of dropping the book with her excited jump.

"This spell can only be used once per full moon," Maddie read slowly.

"Does it say anything else?" Suzanne frowned.

Maddie squinted and angled the book under the light so all the bottom of the page was illuminated. "Yes – this spell cannot be used on the day after the full moon." She stared at Suzanne.

"That's why it didn't work on Walt!" Suzanne's eyes widened.

"I wonder why that note was hidden, though," Maddie mused, placing the heavy book on the bed.

"Yep, that's weird." Suzanne nodded, her ponytail swishing. "But Trixie knew, didn't you?" she smiled at the cat.

"Mrrow." The feline looked pleased at the praise.

"You're so clever, Trix." Maddie bent and patted the Persian. "I just wish we knew why that information was invisible. Did the person who wrote the book want people to fail using the Tell the Truth spell?"

"Ooh, maybe they didn't want that spell to fall into the wrong hands!" Suzanne's face was alive with excitement. "What if they were worried their enemy was going to steal the book, so they wrote that information about the spell in invisible ink, so their enemy would be at a disadvantage if they tried it more than once per full moon – or the day after the full moon, like you did?"

"Maybe," Maddie said thoughtfully. Then she sighed. "I guess we'll never know."

"I wonder if any of the other spells have invisible ink addendums," Suzanne said.

"I guess every time I want to try a spell, I'll have to come in here and check the page with my bedside lamp."

"We better test the Escape your Enemy spell right now!" Suzanne picked up the book.

"You're right." Maddie paged through the book until she found the spell, then she and Suzanne held the book up to the light, but no invisible writing appeared on the page.

"Nothing." Maddie blew out a sigh.

"You're right." Suzanne's tone held a note of disappointment.

"Broomf," Trixie joined in.

"So," Suzanne's tone brightened slightly, "I guess this means you can cast the Escape your Enemy spell anytime you want!" She giggled. "You could try it out the next time you run into Claudine."

"You mean when she runs into me. She's the one always coming over to the coffee truck."

"You're right." Suzanne furrowed her brow. "I just wish she'd stop."

"Me too."

"What if there's a spell in there you can use to make that happen?"

Why hadn't Maddie thought of that?

"Good idea. But I think I'll wait until after the killer is caught. Then I'll – we'll – have plenty of time to look for that kind of spell." Maddie couldn't immediately think of a spell that would discourage Claudine from coming over to Brewed from the Bean and annoying them.

"You're right," Suzanne agreed. "We shouldn't get too distracted. After all, we've got a killer to catch!"

# CHAPTER 14

On Friday morning between serving customers, Maddie and Suzanne discussed what they should do next as they looked through the newspaper. They'd bought it early, and now they finally had time to read Maddie's interview.

"There it is." Suzanne tapped the page. There was a double spread with photos of the contestants from the coffee festival – Claudine was featured, too.

"You sound really good," Suzanne remarked as she read the article.

"Thanks," Maddie replied, reading her answers to the questions Walt had given her. There was only a small mention of the death of Dave Dantzler the radio host at the bottom of the page, and thankfully, no mention in Maddie's feature that she'd been implicated in any way in the crime.

"Walt knows what he's doing," Suzanne said, as she put the newspaper to one side. "He must be a good reporter."

"You're right." Maddie nodded. Somehow, Walt had made her – and the other contestants he'd interviewed – sound like brilliant baristas – even Claudine!

She stifled a yawn as she and Suzanne considered their next move. Last night, Maddie had been unable to settle after Suzanne had gone home, and had carefully paged through *Wytchcraft for the Chosen*, although no spells had tugged at her, finally closing the ancient book when her eyes felt like tiny slits and she could barely see the handwritten words on the page. She'd almost fallen asleep on the sofa until Trixie had nudged her awake and escorted her to bed, curling up beside her.

"I think we should consider the staff at the radio station," Suzanne declared, taking a sip of bottled water.

"And I think we should concentrate on the judge first," Maddie countered. "Let's try to clear the coffee people now, and then if we think everyone is innocent, visit the radio station."

"I guess that makes sense," Suzanne conceded. She glanced at her watch. "Don't forget I've got an appointment with Ramon this afternoon."

"How could I?" Maddie teased. "Three o'clock, right?"

"Right." A dreamy expression flickered across Suzanne's face. "Only five hours to go."

"So if we're going to interview the judge, we better make a plan."

"We could close now, go see him, and get back in time for lunch," Suzanne suggested.

Maddie was about to agree, when she stilled. Walking across the green lawn toward the truck was the very person they'd just spoken of!

"He's here!" She hissed to Suzanne.

"Who?" Suzanne looked puzzled for a second, then her face brightened. "Ramon?"

"No, the judge!"

"Oh!"

"Hello, Ms. Goodwell - Maddie. And Ms. Taylor." Edward Grenville smiled at them.

"Hi, Mr. Grenville," Suzanne greeted him. She slid Maddie a sidelong look. "What can we do for you?"

"I'll have a large latte." He pulled some cash out of his wallet.

Maddie set to work, bringing the hissing espresso machine to life.

Now that the judge was here, her mind had gone blank! What should she ask him? She hoped Suzanne had some questions in mind – her friend was in the best position to assess his reactions to their questions, as Maddie had to focus on making his latte.

"Are you going to be judging the Seattle competition next month?" Suzanne asked.

"Regretfully, no," the judge replied as Maddie foamed milk. "These days, I enjoy the grassroots competitions, such as the one here last weekend."

"Why is that?" Suzanne asked innocently.

"Oh, you know. Getting older, taking time to enjoy the simple pleasures of life."

Maddie finished making the coffee and slid it across the counter to him. "Here you go."

"Thank you." He lifted the paper cup to his lips and sipped. "Ahh, ambrosia. Your cappuccino was the best by far last weekend and I was happy to award you first prize. And now, it seems, your latte is just as good."

"Thank you." Maddie smiled, pleased at his compliment. She only hoped he was innocent, and the praise was truly meant.

"It was terrible about Dave Dantzler being killed at the festival," Suzanne said, watching his expression.

"Yes, of course," the judge replied, but his tone didn't reveal a hint of sorrow.

"Had you met him before?" Maddie asked, remembering what Walt the newspaper reporter had told them – that, on his show, Dave Dantzler had accused the judge of taking bribes.

"Yes." The judge took another sip of his latte.

Maddie and Suzanne exchanged a look. It seemed that questioning this suspect would be more difficult than they thought.

"I don't know if Maddie's interview with him will be heard on the radio station now," Suzanne tried again. "And we were excited about it, weren't we, Maddie?"

"Yes," Maddie replied.

Mr. Grenville tsked. "You're probably better off not appearing on his show," he told them. "Believe me."

Before they could ask him anything more, a *beep beep* filled the air.

The judge looked at his watch. "Time for my pill." He dug into his jacket pocket and pulled out a little pill box. "I have to take these on time or else." He grimaced as he patted his chest.

Maddie's eyes widened as she spied a small heart embossed on the lid of the box. The judge swallowed a tiny pill, washing it down with large sips of his latte.

One idea after another raced through Maddie's mind. A shrill old-fashioned telephone ring cut through the air before she could say anything.

"Now what?" The judge frowned as he pulled his phone from his pocket. He nodded goodbye to them and with his cell phone to his ear, headed toward the other side of the town square.

"Did you see what I saw?" Suzanne asked in an excited tone.

"The heart picture on his pill box?"

"Yes! What if he's the killer?"

"Shh. We don't want anyone to overhear." Maddie craned her head but didn't see anyone in the vicinity. Thank goodness.

"Detective Edgewater said Dave died of a digoxin overdose," Suzanne continued, her voice lower. "What if the judge killed him because of that radio interview last year?"

"The one that Walt the newspaper reporter told us about – Dave tarnished the judge's reputation by accusing him of taking bribes?"

"Yes!"

"Maybe that's why he's not judging big competitions anymore, just like Walt said," Maddie said thoughtfully.

"It's got to be him!" Suzanne insisted. "Who else takes heart medication and was at the festival?"

"Maybe several other people," Maddie pointed out, trying not to get too carried away.

So far, all the clues pointed to Mr. Grenville, the judge, but they couldn't question everyone who'd been at the festival to discover if any of them had a heart condition. For a start, they didn't know all the people who'd attended.

"It's got to be someone connected to Dave in some way. Why would a random stranger kill him?"

"You've got a point," Maddie conceded.

"So let's call Detective Edgewater and tell him what we've found out." Suzanne whipped out her cell phone. "He mightn't know that the judge from the coffee festival is on heart medication."

***

Suzanne shoved the phone back in her pocket. "Detective Edgewater is out in the field," she mimicked a high-pitched voice. "And no, I cannot forward your call to him."

"She was only doing her job," Maddie tried to calm down her friend.

"Or helping the murderer get away!" Suzanne's expression was fierce.

"It's not that bad," Maddie said. "We'll try calling him again later. And if the judge is guilty, it doesn't look like he's making a getaway. He bought a latte from us, after all."

"Don't you think it's suspicious he knew our coffee was safe to drink?" Suzanne snapped her fingers. "That's because he's the killer!"

"Or because he heard that Dave Dantzler was killed by digoxin and not by my coffee," Maddie pointed out.

"Maybe. But on the bright side, at least we know that Bob is innocent."

"There is that," Maddie replied.

"And I still think Jill and Bob would make a cute couple," Suzanne insisted. "When this is all over, if they haven't gotten together, I'm going to see what I can do."

***

When it was almost three o'clock, Suzanne headed across the town square for her massage with Ramon.

That left Maddie on her own in the truck, but she didn't mind. Business was pretty quiet, but it gave her time to tidy up the small interior, and even make a new batch of health balls.

The healthy morsels were Suzanne's domain, but she'd shown Maddie how to make them in case they needed to make more in a hurry.

Just as she put the new batch of maple macadamia in the small fridge to set, Detective Edgewater appeared at the serving hatch.

"Miss Goodwell," he boomed, his face creasing into a smile. "Can you make me a cappuccino?" At his choice of words, he grimaced. "Sorry."

"No problem," she replied, getting the coffee underway. She and Suzanne had recently converted the detective to her cappuccinos, but he'd refused to try anything else.

Now that she knew that Dave hadn't died from her coffee, the thought of making a cappuccino didn't make her shudder any more.

"Shot of vanilla syrup?" she asked as she foamed the milk.

"Yep." He nodded.

"We're out of health balls right now," she told him. "I've got some setting in the fridge though, if you really need one."

"I'll pass this time." He patted his wallet. "I'm trying to cut down on expenses right now."

"Sure." Maddie smiled, wondering how much money he'd spent at their coffee truck since they'd first crossed paths with him a month ago.

"The station told me someone tried to call me earlier today," he said as Maddie slid his drink over to him and took his payment.

"That was Suzanne," she replied, pleased at the opening he'd given her. "We wanted to tell you that the judge, Mr. Grenville, stopped by our truck today and we noticed that he takes heart medication."

"Does he now?" The detective raised his eyebrow. "How do you know?"

"His watch went off and he took a pill, and indicated it was for his heart," Maddie replied.

"I'll look into it," the detective promised. "Do you know how many people take heart medication with digoxin in it?"

Maddie shook her head.

"A lot. Even if his heart medication does contain the substance that killed Mr. Dantzler, that doesn't necessarily mean he's guilty."

"But what about his motive?" Maddie protested. She wished Suzanne was here to lend her voice to the argument.

"What about it?" The detective frowned. "We've got a lot of leads to chase down. Everyone seemed to have a problem with Mr. Dantzler."

Maddie didn't doubt it, if he'd behaved to other people the way he'd behaved to her.

"We were told that Dave Dantzler falsely accused the judge of taking bribes on his show," Maddie informed Detective Edgewater.

"Who told you that?"

Before Maddie could answer, his phone rang, a deep vibrating, *Brrinng! Brrinng!*

The detective looked at his phone. "I've got to take this. I'll look into the judge," he promised, before grabbing his vanilla cappuccino and striding away.

Maddie sighed. She didn't think the detective had seemed very interested in her piece of information about the judge. She just hoped Suzanne was having a better time right now than she was.

# CHAPTER 15

Suzanne came back to Brewed from the Bean positively glowing.

"Mads, you've got to have a massage with Ramon. It's the best!"

"Maybe when this is all over." Perhaps by then she'd be brave enough to allow Ramon's sexy hands and voice work their magic.

"Can you imagine if I was married to him?" Suzanne's tone became soft. "I could have an awesome massage every day."

"I guess that's one reason to marry someone," Maddie teased.

"There are plenty more reasons to marry Ramon," Suzanne joked in return, before slowly turning serious.

"So what should we do now?" Suzanne checked her watch. It was just after four o'clock, and they usually closed the truck at that time. "Try Detective Edgewater again?"

"I forgot to tell you. He stopped by the truck while you were with Ramon. I told him about the judge taking heart medication and what Walt the newspaper reporter told us, about Dave accusing the judge of taking bribes, but then Detective Edgewater got a phone call and had to leave. He said he'd look into it, though."

"Phooey!" Suzanne shook her head. "I'm sure the judge is guilty. Maybe there's another spell in the book you can do to check whether someone is innocent or guilty. Totally different from the Tell the Truth spell."

"Maybe," Maddie said slowly. She couldn't remember such a spell off the top of her head, but they could go back to her place and look through *Wytchcraft for the Chosen* to doublecheck.

"What's Trixie doing?" Suzanne asked as they started closing up the truck.

Maddie fished out her phone and tapped the screen.

"Napping next to the book." She showed Suzanne the screen. The fluffy white Persian dozed peacefully on the sofa, curled up to the ancient tome.

"Ohhhh." Suzanne's tone was soft. "In my next life I want to be a cat *just like Trixie*."

"Me too." Maddie smiled at her friend, but wondered if she'd be happier being a cat who wasn't a familiar.

They drove the truck back to Maddie's house, then trooped inside her cottage. Trixie ran to greet them, although ten minutes ago she'd looked fast asleep on the sofa. How did she do that? Maddie wondered. Had she heard them pull up outside? Or did she use her cat's sixth sense to know the second she and Suzanne arrived?

The three of them settled on the sofa, Maddie and Suzanne on separate sides of the book, and Trixie nestled in Maddie's lap.

"We're looking for a spell to find out if someone is innocent or guilty of a crime, Trix," Maddie told the cat.

"And that's different from the Tell the Truth spell," Suzanne added.

"Mrrow." Trixie looked thoughtful, then peered at the book. She yawned, then promptly re-settled herself in Maddie's lap, looking as if she was going to have another snooze.

"Huh," Suzanne said.

"Yeah," Maddie kept her voice low, so as not to disturb Trixie. "I guess that means there isn't such a spell in the book."

At Suzanne's frown, she continued, "But we can still check."

"Nothing," Suzanne said glumly a while later.

"Uh-huh," Maddie agreed. Trixie still slumbered on her lap.

"I guess Trixie was right."

Maddie nodded.

Suzanne stood. "I still think the judge did it. He had motive, means, and opportunity. Don't forget Bob told us he saw him talking to Dave Dantzler before he announced you as the winner of the competition."

"True," Maddie agreed.

"And we've spoken to the other suspects on our list. I don't think any of them did it. And Detective Edgewater has cleared that middle-aged couple we didn't meet."

"Yes," Maddie said.

"So I think we should march down to the station and tell Detective Edgewater that he should bring in the judge for questioning."

"Maybe we can *suggest* to the detective that he brings in the judge for questioning," Maddie replied.

"Whatever." Suzanne blew out a breath. "I just want to get this murder all wrapped up, you know? Then we can go back to normal – except you'll need to start practicing for the Seattle competition."

"I haven't forgotten." Just the thought of competing with all those accomplished baristas made her feel a little sick with nerves. But the competition was a big opportunity for her – and Suzanne and Trixie. She didn't want to let anyone down.

"Okay, let's go down to the station right now and tell Detective Edgewater what we think."

Maddie gently placed Trixie from her lap onto the sofa, stroking the feline's fur. The cat barely stirred.

"Maybe this week has tired her out more than we realized," Maddie murmured as they grabbed their purses and headed toward the front door.

It was a short drive to the sheriff's station – Maddie felt lazy at taking the car, but right now, it was the most convenient option.

She followed Suzanne into the station, hoping her friend wouldn't just barge in there and demand to see Detective Edgewater.

They were about to ask the sheriff's deputy at the desk if they could speak to the detective when the investigator came barreling out of one of the offices.

"Detective Edgewater!" Suzanne snagged his attention.

"Can't stop now," the detective called out, not lessening his stride. "I just got word the judge has been in a car accident!"

Maddie and Suzanne stared at each other, their eyes wide.

"It looks like we were on the right track, Mads."

***

They followed Detective Edgewater out of the station. "He's at the hospital," the detective informed them tersely. "I'm going there now to interview him."

Maddie nodded, glancing sideways at Suzanne. She appeared as if she were about to say something to the investigator, but Maddie gently touched her arm, giving her a meaningful look.

They watched the detective drive away.

"If he's going to interview the judge, then that means he's alive," Suzanne surmised. "And hopefully not too badly injured."

"We can call the hospital and find out," Maddie said, tapping the buttons on her phone. Once she found the number, she dialed, waiting for someone to respond.

After quickly ascertaining that Maddie and Suzanne were neither family nor friends, they were told that they were not entitled to any information on that patient.

"It looks like we'll have to go over there ourselves," Suzanne said when Maddie ended the call.

"But will they let us see him?" Maddie wondered aloud. "Since we're not family – or friends."

"But he's one of our customers," Suzanne argued. "He stopped by today and bought a latte. I bet if we go to the hospital, and ask to see him, they won't even check if we're actual friends."

"Maybe," Maddie replied. "But we should let Detective Edgewater talk to him first. We don't want to get in his way."

"I suppose," Suzanne conceded. "But what do we do now?"

"How about we go home and talk things over?" Maddie held up her car key. "And see what Trixie's up to?"

"Good idea." Suzanne smiled. "Trixie can always cheer me up."

"It sounds like Ramon can, too," Maddie teased.

"You have *no* idea." Suzanne giggled.

# CHAPTER 16

When they arrived back at Maddie's house, she made a quick dinner of pasta and prepared meatballs for herself and Suzanne. Trixie ate her meal of beef and liver with quiet satisfaction.

"I was so certain it was the judge," Suzanne said once they'd eaten. "But now, with the car accident …"

"Exactly," Maddie replied. That thought had been troubling her on the short journey home. "What if it wasn't an accident? What if the person who killed Dave Dantzler just tried to kill the judge?"

"But why?" Suzanne wrinkled her nose. "Do you think Mr. Grenville knows more than he's letting on?"

"Or maybe the killer thinks that."

The two of them stared at each other.

"Yeah!" Suzanne nodded her head, her ponytail bobbing. "The murderer must have thought he was in danger in some way from Mr. Grenville and decided to silence him."

"Except it didn't work – I don't think," Maddie said. "Because Mr. Grenville is still alive."

"We won't know for sure until we visit him in the hospital." Suzanne scraped back her kitchen chair and paced the room. "I think we should go and visit him right now."

Maddie checked her watch. It was over an hour since Detective Edgewater had left for the hospital. Surely he would have finished questioning the judge by now?"

"Okay," she replied. "But I think we should check what the visiting hours are first. There's no point going over there tonight if it's too late for visitors."

"Agreed."

Maddie glanced at Trixie as she called the hospital. The Persian was finishing her meal, licking her lips with obvious enjoyment – and seemingly oblivious to the conversation. Did that mean she and Suzanne didn't have to worry about the judge coming to harm while in the hospital?

She really wished there was a spell in *Wytchcraft for the Chosen* that would allow her to speak and understand cat.

After talking to a hospital staff member, Maddie ended the call. "Visiting hours are until eight tonight."

"Let's go!" Suzanne grabbed her purse. "We can just make it there in time."

"You stay here, Trixie," Maddie told the cat, who was wandering into the living room, appearing uninterested for once in the goings on.

"I wonder why Trixie isn't curious about the situation," Suzanne said once they were in Maddie's car.

"I know," she agreed as they drove to the hospital. "All I can think of is there isn't any immediate danger, and nothing in the book to help us right now."

They arrived at the hospital with seven minutes to spare. After being directed to the correct wing, they slowed their pace once they reached the right hallway, the beige and white painted walls adding to the blandness of the building.

"I don't think we should barge in there," Maddie murmured to Suzanne as they approached room 319. The smell of disinfectant stung her nostrils.

"Okay," Suzanne said reluctantly, glancing at her watch. "We only have four minutes, though."

Maddie knocked on the partly open door. "Hello?" she called out.

A passing nurse frowned at them as she walked past in rubber soled shoes. "Visiting hours are almost over."

"We know." Suzanne flashed her a smile. "We only just found out about—"

"Don't be long," the nurse admonished them, as she passed them.

"Phew!" Suzanne muttered under her breath.

"Come in." A low male voice called out to them.

Maddie pushed open the door and smiled tentatively at the judge. He sat in bed with the sheets pulled up to his waist and sported a large white dressing on the side of his forehead.

"Hi, Mr. Grenville," Maddie said. "We heard you were in an accident and—"

"We wanted to see how you were," Suzanne jumped in.

"That's nice of you," he said, closing his eyes, as if tired. "I've got broken ribs, and this." He pointed to the bandage on his head. "Ms. Goodwell and Ms. Taylor, right?"

"Do you know who did this to you?" Suzanne asked eagerly.

"No one." He shook his head and then winced.

"What do you mean?" Maddie asked.

"It was my own stupid fault." He grimaced. "Nearly every time I've braked lately when driving the car, I've heard a squeaking noise. I thought it was dust in the brakes and I'd get around to taking it to the mechanic when I had time."

"What happened?" Suzanne asked.

"I was rounding a corner and the brakes failed." He shook his head, the movement making him wince again. "I crashed into that large pine tree on the corner of Basin Road. Do you know it?"

"Yes," Maddie replied, thinking the judge was lucky he was still alive.

"If only I hadn't put off getting the brakes checked out."

"But how do you know it was … natural causes?" Suzanne asked, leaning forward. "Maybe someone cut your brake lines."

"Suzanne!" Maddie whispered.

"Why would anyone do that?" The judge looked puzzled.

"Because you know something and the killer knows you know something," Suzanne informed him.

"Killer?" He frowned. "Oh, you mean whoever murdered Dave Dantzler."

"Yes!"

Suzanne seemed to have gone from insisting the judge was guilty to acting like he was innocent. But, Maddie had to concede, his car accident did seem a strange coincidence.

"We were told Dave falsely accused you on his radio show," Maddie said delicately.

"Yes." Mr. Grenville sank back against the pillows. "It's true, he did accuse me of taking bribes when I appeared on his show last year. He didn't care about the truth – just about his ratings."

"What happened?" Maddie asked gently, exchanging a look with Suzanne.

"He wouldn't allow me to explain what had really happened. I was exonerated years ago. It was actually another judge on the coffee circuit who had been taking bribes. When he was discovered, he fled to another state – Maine, I think." He waved a hand. "It was in the newspapers at the time – you can check. Once the truth came out, my reputation mostly recovered, but when Dave raked it all up again last year, I couldn't believe it."

"What did you do?" Suzanne held her breath, waiting for his answer.

"Nothing." He let out a short, mirthless laugh. "The damage had been done, and this time it's lasted. These days, people aren't interested in researching allegations to find out if they're even true. They prefer to believe whoever is casting aspersions on another person, even when it's scurrilous lies. So I found myself not being asked to judge major coffee competitions anymore, even though the local newspaper printed the truth."

"That must have been disappointing," Suzanne sympathized.

"Yes." Mr. Grenville looked exhausted. "The only bright side – if you can call it that – was that I'd been thinking of slowing down my schedule anyway, preparatory to retirement. But that decision was taken out of my hands." He sighed. "Now I'm lucky to be invited to judge competitions such as the one you won, Maddie."

"I'm sorry," Maddie said, her tone sincere.

"It was kind of you to visit me," he said, closing his eyes once more. "But I'm afraid I'm very tired. Would you think it rude of me if I wanted to rest now?"

"Of course not," Suzanne and Maddie said together.

"Take care," Maddie added, as they walked quietly out of the room. She pulled the door shut after them.

"Poor man." Suzanne shook her head as they walked down the hallway.

"I know."

"But—" Suzanne grabbed Maddie's arm. "What if those brakes were cut? And what if he cut them himself?"

"Why would he do that?" Maddie crinkled her brow.

“To divert suspicion away from himself,” Suzanne declared.

“And risk killing himself at the same time?” Maddie’s tone was skeptical.

“We don’t know what goes through a killer’s mind,” Suzanne told her. “Hey!” She lowered her voice. “Did you try the Tell the Truth spell on him in there?”

“No,” Maddie admitted. She’d been so caught up in the judge’s explanation that it hadn’t crossed her mind. “He seemed honest and sincere to me.”

“I know.” Suzanne blew out a breath and started walking down the hallway. “I really felt sorry for him in there, and I thought I believed what he said. And then when we came out of the room and I thought about brakes and how someone could cut them, I thought what if …?”

“Sometimes thinking that way can be dangerous,” Maddie told her as they reached the parking lot.

“Yeah.”

Maddie pulled out of the parking lot and headed home. When she pressed on the brakes, she was relieved to find they didn’t squeak.

"If your brakes start squeaking, you better get them checked out ASAP." Suzanne's voice broke the silence. "Just in case a squeak means worn brake pads."

"Exactly what I was just thinking," Maddie replied, glad they'd be home in a few minutes.

When she parked outside her house, she turned to Suzanne. "Want to come in?"

"Thanks, but I better head home." She yawned, her hand covering her mouth. "The first thing I'm going to do tomorrow is call Detective Edgewater and find out what really happened to the judge's car – whether the brake line was cut, or if it really was natural wear and tear."

# CHAPTER 17

The next morning, Maddie watched Suzanne attempt to call Detective Edgewater between coffee orders.

Trixie sat on her stool in the early morning sun, lazily waving a paw to her favorite customers.

Their Saturday morning rush was in full swing, with customers gobbling up two varieties of health balls – maple macadamia and cacao coconut.

"Finally!" Suzanne muttered as she held her cell phone to her ear. Maddie could hear the faint sound of ringing on the other end of the line.

Maddie heard her friend's part of the conversation as she made a large vanilla latte for an elderly man, smiling at him as she handed him the drink and taking his money, while Suzanne was occupied.

"Okay, detective. Thanks." Suzanne ended the call. "He said he's going to come over and tell us what happened last night to the judge. Oh, and he asked for a large vanilla cappuccino and two health balls, ready to go."

"Okay." Maddie set to work, making the detective's favorite drink.

Suzanne practically hopped with impatience as she waited for Detective Edgewater to arrive. When he finally lumbered into view, she rushed to the serving window. Luckily, there were no other customers around, so the three of them could talk in relative privacy.

"Here you go, detective." Maddie handed him the large paper cup and a small bag holding the health balls. They'd decided to give him one of each flavor, since he hadn't specified on the phone.

"Thanks." He took a sip of the coffee, his face creasing into a smile. "I'm glad you won that competition, Miss Goodwell. You deserved to."

"Thanks." Maddie smiled.

"That's seven ninety, please." Suzanne held out her hand for the money.

"No wonder you girls make a living at this." He mock-grumbled, pulling out some bills from his wallet.

"Now tell us what happened to the judge's car," Suzanne urged.

Trixie sat up straight on her stool, her ears pricked.

The detective took the demand in a good-humored manner.

"No foul play was involved last night," he pronounced after another sip of his coffee. "Those brake pads were worn away." He tsked. "If you ever hear your brakes squeak, you better get them checked out ASAP."

"We will," Maddie vowed.

"It was lucky he wasn't injured more severely," the detective continued. "That tree will never be the same, though, on Basin Road. They're talking about cutting it down."

"Oh." Maddie had often walked past the huge pine tree, marveling at its height and strong proportions.

"So there was no possibility his brakes could have been tampered with?" Suzanne doublechecked.

"None at all," Detective Edgewater reassured her.

"But what about his heart medication?" Suzanne persisted. "If his car crash last night was an accident, he could have still slipped Dave Dantzler an overdose of digoxin in his coffee." She frowned at the detective. "Was Dave on heart medication? You haven't told us yet."

He sighed. "No, he wasn't. And I looked into Mr. Grenville, the judge, Miss Taylor. He's on a medication that contains nitroglycerine, not digoxin. So he appears to be in the clear. We'll be focusing our inquiries in other areas."

"Oh," Maddie said. She was pleased that it looked like the judge was innocent – she'd taken a liking to the man – but where did that leave their investigation? Hers and Suzanne's – and Trixie's?

# CHAPTER 18

"It must be someone from the radio station," Suzanne declared when Detective Edgewater had departed.

"You could be right," Maddie agreed.

"Mrrow?" Trixie inquired.

"Do you want to come with us to the radio station, Trixie?" Suzanne leaned down and spoke to the cat.

"Mrrow!" Trixie tilted her head, as if liking the idea of another outing.

"This afternoon?" Maddie suggested. "We'll be closing at lunchtime today."

"Perfect!"

"Do you think they'll have staff who work there on the weekend?" Maddie posed the question.

"They must have," Suzanne said. "Although, if the right person isn't there to talk to us, we can go back on Monday. But at least we're doing something about it."

"By *it,* I suppose you mean unmasking the killer."

"Yep."

Another wave of customers stopped by. When they departed, Suzanne turned to Maddie. "Are you going to cast the Coffee Vision spell today?"

"I guess." So much had happened since last weekend – was it really only a week since the coffee festival? – that she hadn't felt compelled to cast the Coffee Vision spell for herself, Suzanne, or her customers.

"It might help us with our visit to the radio station this afternoon," Suzanne suggested.

"Okay." Maddie made herself a mocha, staring into the microfoam. She focused her mind, the presence of Suzanne and Trixie receding to the background. "Show me," she whispered.

The foam swirled, then cleared. An image of herself, Suzanne, and Trixie in an office appeared on the surface of the coffee. A lady in her sixties was petting Trixie and making a fuss of her, something that the cat seemed to be enjoying.

"Well?" Suzanne asked eagerly when Maddie blinked and returned to the present.

"What did you see?"

"Not much," she confessed, rapidly filling in Suzanne on her vision.

"Oh." Suzanne seemed a little disappointed. "At least it looks like Trixie will be enjoying herself this afternoon, though."

"Mrrow!" Trixie agreed.

Maddie and Suzanne closed the truck at lunchtime, Suzanne hopping with impatience. They drove the truck back to Maddie's house, then grabbed her car.

"I don't think I've ever visited the radio station," Suzanne said as they drove to the edge of town. Trixie sat in the back seat, glancing through the closed window with interest, looking cute in her turquoise harness. Maddie periodically checked on her through the rear-view mirror.

"Me neither," Maddie agreed, as they neared the one-story brown brick building. She parked in the visitor's lot.

"How are we going to play this?" Suzanne asked as they walked toward the entrance.

"We could tell them we're sorry to hear about Dave's death and that we were wondering if my interview will go ahead some time in the future?" Maddie suggested.

"Good idea." Suzanne nodded.

They opened the glass entrance door and walked inside. An unmanned reception desk faced them.

Maddie and Suzanne turned to each other.

"Now what?" Maddie murmured.

But Trixie seemed to know where to go. With a little "Mrrow," she pulled Maddie to the right, down a short hallway.

"Well, hello there, little one." A woman in her sixties with short, silvery hair greeted Trixie.

Maddie stilled. It was the woman from the Coffee Vision spell! Although she'd been casting this spell for twenty years, she never failed to be surprised when she met the person she'd seen in an image on the surface of a freshly brewed coffee, especially if that person was a stranger.

Trixie purred and tilted her head up to the elderly lady, as if inviting the woman to stroke her.

"Oh, hello." The woman smiled at Maddie and Suzanne. "I didn't see you there at first. I was too busy looking at this little one."

"She has that effect on people," Maddie said wryly. "Her name is Trixie."

"What a pretty name for a pretty cat," the senior cooed at Trixie. The feline lapped up the attention, chirping a happy "Mrrow" at the woman.

"I'm Maddie and this is Suzanne," Maddie introduced themselves.

"We wanted to stop by and say we were sorry about Dave's death," Suzanne jumped in.

The woman tsked. "It was terrible. Oh, I didn't introduce myself." She looked a little flustered. "I'm Judy."

"We didn't see a receptionist when we came in," Suzanne said. "Trixie led us here."

"She was right." Judy smiled down at the cat. "We have a skeleton staff on the weekends. Apart from the radio hosts, I'm usually the only employee on duty."

"We were wondering if Maddie's interview would be played on the station one day," Suzanne said innocently. "You see, Dave interviewed her last Saturday at the coffee festival. She won the competition and will be competing in the big Seattle competition next month."

"Congratulations." The senior beamed at them.

"Thank you," Maddie replied.

"I'll have to come and try your coffee one day. Where are you?"

"We operate Brewed from the Bean at the town square in Estherville," Suzanne informed her. "Monday to Friday 7am 'til 4, and Saturdays 7.30 'til lunchtime."

Maddie frowned at Suzanne. Her friend sounded like a TV or radio ad!

"Oh, you're not far from the library," Judy said. "I've got some books I need to return next week, so I'll stop in then."

"We'll look forward to it." Suzanne grinned. "And we have health balls too – they're morsels of wholesome ingredients that taste so delicious, they don't seem healthy at all!"

Maddie raised an eyebrow in Suzanne's direction. Sometimes her friend could go a little overboard in recommending their coffee to others.

Suzanne must have received the unspoken message though, as she became silent.

"That sounds wonderful." The senior smiled. "I can't wait to stop by."

Trixie rubbed against the older woman's legs, covered in a pair of gray slacks, glancing at Maddie, and then concentrating on leaving her scent on Judy. Was Trixie trying to tell Maddie something? Should she use the Tell the Truth spell?

She fingered the spell in her purse. A calmness descended as she focused. The words appeared in her mind. Silently, she uttered them, whispering, "Show me," at the end.

"Will you have a replacement host for the radio show?" Maddie asked.

"Yes, they're interviewing next week," Judy informed them. "Until then, hosts with their own shows are filling in the time slot."

A deep knowing filled Maddie. Judy told the truth!

"Maddie was interviewed by the newspaper reporter, too," Suzanne mentioned. "But her interview was bumped to yesterday because of what happened."

"Oh, was that Walt?" the senior asked. As they nodded, she continued, "I remember him. He interviewed for this job a couple of years ago. He seemed like such a nice man! And a good reporter, too. But they gave it to Dave instead." She tsked, then looked around, although the hallway was empty. "I did hear a rumor that Dave blackmailed someone to get the job, but it's only a rumor."

Maddie and Suzanne stared at each other, then Maddie glanced down at Trixie, who looked pleased with herself. Was that what the Persian wanted them to know?

"That's terrible." Maddie found her voice.

"I know," the senior mourned. "I shouldn't be saying this, but Dave wasn't a nice man to work with. Very demanding."

"Do you know who he blackmailed?" Maddie asked.

"No." Judy shook her head. "As I said, it was only a rumor, although it did sound like it was someone in upper management who had the power to hire someone for that slot."

"Maybe we should talk to him," Suzanne said slowly.

"No one in upper management will be here until Monday morning," Judy informed them. "Let me see—" she appeared to be thinking "—yes, we have two executives and they were both working here when Dave was hired. If you want to know more, then you could come back next week when they'll be in."

"We will," Suzanne promised.

They said goodbye to Judy, the older woman making a fuss of Trixie before they departed, then they walked back to the entrance, Trixie leading the way in her turquoise harness, her plumy silver tail waving in the air.

"Good job we came here," Suzanne remarked as they got into Maddie's car. "What if it is someone from the radio station? Maybe Dave wasn't satisfied with his salary – maybe he decided to turn up the heat and continue to blackmail one of the executives into giving him a pay rise!"

"It's possible." Maddie touched Suzanne's arm. "I cast the Tell the Truth spell, and it worked! Judy was definitely telling the truth about Dave – or at least, what she knew to be the truth."

"That's great!" Suzanne grinned.

"Mrrow!"

"So, what do you want to do now?" Suzanne asked as Maddie drove out of the parking lot.

"How about visiting Walt at the newspaper office again?" she suggested. "He certainly didn't tell us he once competed with Dave for the same job."

"Yeah!" Suzanne grinned. "This sleuthing is fun!"

"As long as I'm not face to face with a killer again," Maddie cautioned her.

"Don't worry. You've got me and Trixie by your side – and the Escape your Enemy spell." Suzanne peered at her. "You do have it on you, don't you?"

"In my purse," Maddie reassured her friend.

"Mrrow!" Trixie joined in, as if knowing that was where Maddie had put the spell.

"Let's go!"

Maddie parked outside the newspaper office and checked her watch. "It's three o'clock." She turned to Suzanne. "Do you think anyone will still be here?"

"Only one way to find out." Suzanne smiled and hopped out of the car.

Maddie followed, holding onto Trixie's lead as the feline gracefully leaped to the ground. The three of them trooped to the glass entrance door. Maddie tentatively pushed it open.

"There must be someone here." Suzanne entered first.

Maddie and Trixie followed.

"Hello?" Maddie called out when they reached the vacant reception desk.

"Hello??" Suzanne's voice was a little louder.

"Hi." Walt suddenly appeared near reception. "What can I do for you two?" He smiled.

"Is this a bad time?" Maddie asked, feeling a little guilty for interrupting him at work – for the second time.

"No." He shook his head. "I was getting ready to go home, actually. The newspaper's finished for tomorrow. Come on back."

They followed him into the open plan office until they reached his desk. “Take a seat.” He gestured to two visitor chairs near his desk, and sat down on his ergonomic chair. He seemed to be the only employee in the office.

Trixie sniffed at the wastepaper bin next to his desk, the lead on the harness stretched out to its maximum length.

“Sorry,” Maddie apologized.

“No problem.” He smiled at the cat. “She’s a real cutie. Did you get a chance to read your interview in yesterday’s paper?”

“Yes.” Maddie nodded. “Thanks for not saying anything about – you know – Dave Dantzler holding my – our – coffee cup …”

“No problem.”

“It was great,” Suzanne put in. “In fact, you made everyone sound amazing.”

“Thanks.” He looked pleased.

“We were just at the radio station,” Suzanne said. “We wanted to find out if they were still going to play Maddie’s interview, now that Dave is dead.”

"And the employee there told us you competed with Dave for that very job two years ago," Maddie finished in a rush.

"Yeah." Walt nodded. "And I didn't get it." He grimaced.

"Was that because Dave blackmailed one of the station executives into giving him the job?" Suzanne asked innocently.

"Is that what you heard?" Walt's eyes flared.

Maddie nodded.

Walt's mouth twisted. "Yeah, I overheard something after Dave got the job. See, we used to work together, in this office." He gestured at the vacant desks and chairs. "Then the job at the radio station came up. We both applied for it, and I actually thought I had a shot of getting it." He laughed bitterly. "I should have known better."

"What happened?" Maddie asked.

"I was always the better reporter. Dave cut corners whenever he could, said he was meant for better things than just being a beat reporter. But I made sure I checked my facts, got my stories in on time, and thought a good solid work ethic would bring me success in the long run.

Instead, it seems you have to blackmail someone if you want to go places."

"What did he do?" Suzanne held her breath.

"I don't know the full story, but after he came crowing into the office, telling everyone he got the job, before I even heard I'd been unsuccessful, I overheard him on the phone later that day. He seemed to be talking to the guy who actually awarded him the job, one of the radio execs. Dave said he better get a ten percent pay increase every year, or else."

Maddie and Suzanne stared at each other. Dave had not been a nice person at all!

"Why did you apply for the job in the first place?" Maddie asked curiously.

"Better pay," Walt replied. "And I thought it would be fun, interviewing people live on the radio. It was supposed to be a reporter based show, so I'd still be using my skills as a newspaper reporter. But instead, when Dave got the job, he turned the show into a sensationalist news show and didn't bother to check his facts before he accused people of crimes, whether real or imagined. Like the judge who announced you as the winner at the coffee festival, Maddie."

Maddie and Suzanne both nodded.

"Dave loved doing stuff like that, and didn't seem to care who he hurt in the process."

Before Maddie could think of another question to ask him, the landline on Walt's desk rang.

"I'll be home soon, Mom," he spoke into the receiver. "Yes, okay, I'll pick it up for you. Bye." He returned the receiver to its cradle with a soft thunk.

"My mother," he explained unnecessarily.

Maddie glanced at the photo of Walt and his mother on his desk. His arm was around his mother's shoulders.

"She looks like a nice lady," Maddie offered.

"She is." He smiled. "That's another reason why I wanted the radio job. With better pay, I could help her out more. Her medications can be expensive."

His conversation on the phone flitted through Maddie's mind.

"Do you live with her?" she blurted out, immediately embarrassed.

"Yeah." He picked up the photo, showing it to them, the ocean backdrop looking inviting. "I took her on vacation to Hawaii five years ago – that was when she was more mobile." He shook his head. "A while after that it became obvious she needed more help around the house, and it made sense that I moved in with her. And I'd be saving on rent as well."

Maddie studied the photo, once more noticing the pretty silver bracelet. She squinted: was there engraving on it in the shape of a star?

"I guess we should go." Maddie rose, not wanting to bother Walt any longer. "It sounds like your mother needs you."

"She always needs me," he said.

Trixie trotted over to Maddie. The whole time, she'd been investigating the wastepaper basket. Now, she barely gave the reporter a glance.

"I think Trixie wants to go home, too," Suzanne said with a laugh. "Thanks for talking with us."

"My pleasure." He smiled.

They waved goodbye, then hopped into Maddie's car.

"Poor Walt." Suzanne crinkled her brow. "It doesn't seem fair that Dave got the job when it was obvious Walt was the better person."

"Yeah," Maddie agreed. "But look what happened to Dave. Although at first he got away with blackmailing someone to get ahead, it didn't turn out too well for him in the long run."

"Crime does not pay," Suzanne declared.

"Mrrow!" Trixie agreed.

Maddie looked at Trixie sitting on the back seat. The cat had been quiet in the newspaper office, seemingly content to investigate the wastepaper basket. But she hadn't emerged with a piece of paper in her mouth, or something stuck to her fur or paw which could be considered a clue.

She sighed. Was she really cut out for sleuthing? It felt like they'd questioned a ton of people, and still hadn't discovered who killed Dave.

"I think on Monday we should visit the radio station again," Suzanne said as Maddie parked outside her house. "We can go after the morning rush and get back in time for the lunch crowd."

"Do you really think the killer works for the radio station?" Maddie asked with a frown. Something tugged at the back of her mind, but she didn't know what it was. Had she missed something somewhere?

"If he doesn't, then who did it?" Suzanne shrugged. "I'd love for the killer to be Claudine, but I don't think she did it."

"No," Maddie agreed.

They got out of the car and walked up to the house. Maddie unlocked the door and they made their way to the kitchen, Trixie immediately sitting by her food bowl.

"Okay, Trix." Maddie got the sachet of cat food out of the fridge and squeezed it into the dish. Trixie started eating immediately.

"That reminds me." Suzanne touched her forehead. "I'm having dinner with my brother." She checked her watch. "I better get going."

Envy swept through Maddie, which she immediately squelched. "Have a good time."

"I will." Suzanne smiled. "He's paying. He called me last night, asking if I was free but wouldn't tell me what it was about." Her eyes widened and her smile grew bigger. "Oh, I bet I know what it is!"

"What?" Maddie was caught up in her friend's excitement.

"He wants to ask me about you! If you're seeing anyone. I just know it!"

"Do you think?" Maddie tried to tamp down her sudden excitement but lost the battle.

"What else could it be? It's not our parents' birthday or anniversary soon. Why else would he treat me to dinner?"

"Because he's a nice guy?"

"Well, yeah, but … when we catch up, it's usually more planned. Oh, I just know it's going to be about you!" Suzanne looked gleeful. "Don't worry, I'm going to make you sound so irresistible he's not going to have a chance!"

“Suzanne,” Maddie cautioned, “you won’t tell him about—” she swept her hand in the air, indicating first Trixie, and then the living room where *Wytchcraft for the Chosen* lay on the sofa.

“Of course not!” her friend reassured her. “Don’t worry, I promised you a long time ago I would never tell another soul about your abilities and I haven’t.”

“I know. I’m sorry,” Maddie replied.

“Don’t worry, I get it.” Suzanne hugged her. “I’ll come by tomorrow and tell you about dinner, and then we can go through our list of suspects and cross off the ones we know are innocent. And then make a plan for Monday.”

## CHAPTER 19

Maddie spent Saturday night wondering what Suzanne and her brother Luke were talking about over dinner. Was it truly about her? Or was her friend so caught up with matchmaking that she was letting that enthusiasm carry her away?

She watched some TV with Trixie, but couldn't concentrate. Maddie wandered around the house while the cat dozed on the sofa, but she couldn't think of anything to do. Finally, she ended up back on the sofa, slowly looking through *Wytchcraft for the Chosen*, but no spells tugged at her, trying to catch her attention.

Should she do a Coffee Vision spell? Maybe it would show her what would happen tomorrow. But she didn't even feel like making a latte right now. And what if the vision showed her an image of Suzanne's brother?

She didn't think she could deal with that.

Maddie ended up going to bed at 9.30 p.m., half of her wanting to know if Suzanne's brother really was interested in her, and the other half not wanting to know, in case she was doomed to disappointment.

***

On Sunday morning, Maddie forced herself not to think about Suzanne's brother Luke. Instead, she went over the questions they'd asked each suspect. Something still nagged at the back of her mind.

"Do you know, Trix?" she asked the cat, as they sat on the sofa, *Wytchcraft for the Chosen* beside them.

"Mrrow." Trixie looked thoughtful for a moment, then slowly closed her eyes.

Did that mean the Persian did know who the killer was? It wouldn't surprise Maddie if she did. After all, the spell book was real, and so was the Coffee Vision spell and the Truth spell. Only time would tell if the Escape your Enemy spell was real as well.

But if Trixie knew who the killer was, why wasn't she telling her? Or did Maddie have to learn the cat language in order to find out?

*Ding dong*. The doorbell interrupted her musing. Maddie and Trixie headed toward the hall, Trixie scampering to the front door.

Maddie peeked through the peephole – yep, it was Suzanne, looking excited.

"You'll never guess!" She barreled into the house as soon as the door was open wide enough to get through. "Hi, Trixie," she greeted the feline, as she swept down the hall into the kitchen.

Maddie and Trixie followed.

"I was right!" Suzanne crowed, plonking herself down at the kitchen table. "Luke took me to dinner last night to ask all about you!"

"Really?" Maddie's face flamed, while millions of butterflies zoomed and whooshed in her stomach.

"Really!" Suzanne grinned. "It's going to be so good having you as a sister!"

Maddie's mouth parted as she stared at her friend.

"I'm kidding." Suzanne lightly punched Maddie on the arm. "Well, only half kidding. It would be so cool if you and my brother got married one day, but I guess I'm jumping the gun a little."

"A little," Maddie managed to squeak.

"Sit down." Suzanne patted the place at the kitchen table opposite her.

Maddie sat, not sure if her wobbly knees would be able to hold her up any longer.

Trixie sat too, on the kitchen chair next to Maddie, her ears pricked and her expression alert, as if she wanted to hear all the details as well.

"We had dinner at that little place just off the town square. I had the pork ribs and he had the steak with Portobello mushrooms. Oh, those ribs were so delicious, we'll have to go there one night. And then he told me about how he's been so swamped with work—"

"Suzanne," Maddie interrupted. "Are you sure he asked about me?"

"I'm getting to it." Suzanne waved her hand as if she thought Maddie was being a tad impatient. "It's important to set the scene. So, he was telling me how swamped he's been at work, but he hasn't been able to stop thinking about you – like, forever! And then he asked me if I thought it would be weird if he asked you out on a date, and what I thought your answer would be. Because he knows we've been best friends since middle school and he didn't want to ruin that, but he said seeing you at the coffee festival and then again last week, just made him realize how much he likes you and—"

"He likes me?"

"Yep." Suzanne's tone was smug. "I should be a matchmaker for real. Anyway, I gave him the green light to go ahead and ask you out. And I said to him, "You better ask her out after you've been talking about her for a whole hour—"

"He talked about me for that long?" Maddie held her breath, waiting for her friend's answer.

"Yep." Suzanne grinned. "Actually, it got kind of boring after a while, because he was telling me things about you that I already know. And I kept thinking, but you don't know that Maddie's a witch!" She giggled.

When Maddie and Trixie stared at her, she shook her head, her ponytail swishing vigorously.

"Don't worry, I didn't breathe a word! You know I wouldn't – ever – to anyone."

"I know," Maddie replied.

"Mrrow," Trixie agreed.

"It was just fun to think about it when he was going on and on about what an amazing barista you are and he was glad he helped us restore the truck when we were first starting out, and if I knew if you were seeing anyone—"

"What did you say?"

"No, of course." Suzanne grinned. "I told him he should help you practice for the Seattle competition."

Maddie shivered with excitement at Suzanne's revelations. But she cautioned herself not to get carried away. Suzanne's brother Luke had had plenty of time to ask her out – years, in fact – so why was he only doing so now?

"Hey," Suzanne said, her voice softer. "I know that pensive look. I asked Luke why he hadn't asked you out before and he finally told me it was because he thought you were special, and he didn't want to mess it up. Or make it weird between us – me and him and you and me." She tsked. "Guys can be strange at times." Her eyes widened as a thought occurred to her. "Ooh, I wonder if he saw Ramon at our truck at the festival? That might have finally compelled him to act!"

Maddie crinkled her brow.

"He might have thought Ramon was interested in you," Suzanne explained.

"But he's not," Maddie pointed out, knowing of her friend's interest in the sexy masseuse.

"I know that – I think. I mean, it's hard to tell with Ramon, he's just so, so—"

"I know." Maddie nodded in agreement.

"Mrrow," Trixie put in.

"But Luke doesn't know that. And," Suzanne added, "I might have told my brother that you were thinking of getting a massage with Ramon."

"Suzanne!" Maddie gasped.

"Well, you are, aren't you?" Suzanne looked satisfied with herself.

"Y-e-s," Maddie admitted, wondering if she'd ever be brave enough.

“So it wasn’t a lie. Sometimes my brother needs something to be spelled out to him, even if it’s right under his nose. And he’d promised he’d call you and ask you out.”

“Really?” Maddie sank back in the kitchen chair, the hard wooden back digging into her shoulder blades.

Trixie looked from Maddie to Suzanne and back again, an inquisitive look on her face.

“Really,” Suzanne confirmed. “And all you have to do is say yes.” She paused. “You are going to say yes, aren’t you?”

“Mrrow!”

“Yes.” Maddie and Trixie spoke at the same time.

“Good.” Suzanne grinned. “You like my brother, don’t you, Trix?”

“Mrrow.” Trixie looked as if she were saying yes.

“Just call me Suzanne the Matchmaker.” The two of them laughed, Trixie joining in with a happy, “Mrrow.”

“Now that’s out of the way,” Suzanne became serious, “we better go through our list of suspects and see who we’ve got left.”

"Okay." Maddie rose and grabbed the list from her purse.

"But first—" Suzanne's gaze cut to the coffee machine on Maddie's kitchen counter. "I'd love a coffee."

Smiling, Maddie made them both a latte from her fancy espresso machine. It was smaller than the machine she used in the truck, but just the right size for home use. And since she made most of her caffeinated drinks at Brewed from the Bean, she didn't need the most expensive appliance to make a decent cup of coffee at home.

Trixie continued to sit at the table, watching as Maddie brought the cups over.

"Let's see." Maddie scanned the list as she sipped her latte. "We've already crossed off the middle-aged couple that Detective Edgewater cleared."

"That's right." Suzanne put down her cup on the table with a small thunk. "And it looks like the judge didn't do it. He doesn't take the right heart medication."

"I know you thought he might have been involved or that the killer thought he knew something after he had the car accident," Maddie replied. "But then Detective Edgewater told us that the judge's brakes failed because of natural wear and tear, nothing to do with someone tampering with them – or even the judge tampering with them because he was the killer and wanted to divert suspicion from himself."

"Right." Suzanne nodded. "So we should cross him off, too."

Maddie slashed a line through the judge's name.

"And there's no way Jill or Bob could have done it." Suzanne insisted.

Maddie hesitated. "Just because someone is nice doesn't mean they're not a killer."

"I know, but I can't see Jill killing Dave. And you said Bob didn't do it." Suzanne sipped her latte, closing her eyes in appreciation. "So good. Just make one of these for my brother every day and he'll be yours forever."

"Suzanne!" Maddie blushed, aware that Trixie was looking at her with interest. Was the Persian taking Suzanne's words literally? "She's just teasing, Trix," Maddie murmured to the cat.

"Teasing, foretelling the future, who knows?" Suzanne winked at Trixie.

"If we could get back to the list of suspects." Maddie cleared her throat. "I'll put a question mark next to Jill."

"Okay." Suzanne looked disappointed, then peered across the table at the suspect list. You didn't put Ramon on the list, did you?"

"No." Maddie shook her head.

"Good. Now, what about Claudine? I wish she was the guilty one, but she's not." Suzanne winkled her nose.

"Yeah." Now it was Maddie's turn to look glum.

"So that leaves Walt."

"Uh-huh." Maddie's pen hovered over the newspaper reporter's name. Something still nagged her about their conversation with him yesterday, but she couldn't put her finger on it – yet.

"He certainly had motive," Suzanne said.

"Yes."

"What was Trixie doing digging in his wastepaper basket while we were talking to him?" Suzanne asked curiously.

"I have no idea." Maddie turned to the cat. "Trix?"

But all Trixie said, was "Mrrow," with an inscrutable look on her face.

Suzanne sighed. "I think we should leave him on the list for now."

"Just what I was going to suggest." Maddie put down the pen.

"So that leaves the two radio execs to interview tomorrow," Suzanne said. "We could go after the lunch rush, maybe."

"Okay," Maddie replied slowly. "But do you really think it's going to be one of them?"

"What if Dave wanted a huge salary increase and the station couldn't afford it?" Suzanne suggested. "And he threatened to reveal the executive's secret, which is why one or both of them killed him."

"Maybe," Maddie said, adding, *two radio executives* on the suspect list.

Suzanne blew out a breath. "But if it's not them, then who could it be? And we need to find out somehow if they're on heart medication or have access to it."

Maddie's pen clattered to the table. Something her friend had just said jogged her memory. What was it? She furrowed her brow but it remained tantalizingly out of reach.

Then she sighed. It was gone.

# CHAPTER 20

Suzanne stayed a while longer, then went home, telling Maddie she'd see her at Brewed from the Bean in the morning.

Maddie kept mentally going over the suspect list, wondering what had teased the edges of her mind. Had it been something Suzanne had said? Something one of the suspects had told them? She tried to puzzle it out, but couldn't come up with anything.

She even paged through *Wytchcraft for the Chosen,* wondering if there was a spell in there – one she hadn't noticed before, or one that might magically appear just when she needed it, to discover who the killer was – but she couldn't find anything like that.

She finally ordered herself to stop thinking about it at eight p.m. Her mind felt like mush.

When the phone rang, she jumped, clapping a hand to her chest.

"I'm being silly," she told Trixie, who had been dozing on the sofa next to the spell book. Trixie blinked awake, staring at the cell phone as a *brring brring* sounded in the living room. Maybe it was Suzanne.

It was Luke, Suzanne's brother.

Maddie sank down on the sofa when she heard his attractive male voice. I'm behaving like a teenager, she scolded herself, attempting to sound unruffled as she composed an answer to his question – would you like to go out on Friday night?

"Yes, I'd love to," she answered, wondering if she'd answered too quickly.

To her surprise, he sounded a little relieved at her answer. They made arrangements for dinner in Estherville, Luke promising to pick her up.

After she ended the call, Maddie realized Trixie had been gazing at her the whole time she'd been talking to Luke.

"He's asked me out – on a date," she unnecessarily told the feline. "We're having dinner."

"Mrrow." Trixie nudged her hand in approval, demanding Maddie pet her.

Maddie thought back over the phone call. Wait until she told Suzanne tomorrow! She hugged herself, then

Trixie. She had a date with her longtime crush for Friday night!

Maddie and Trixie watched some TV, although Maddie found it hard to keep her mind on the family drama. All she wanted to think about was her upcoming date with Luke!

Finally, Maddie forced herself to go to bed. She had to get up at 6.30 a.m. tomorrow so she and Suzanne could open Brewed from the Bean at 7.30.

She and Trixie curled up in bed, Maddie under the blankets, and Trixie on top, in the crook of her knees. Just as Maddie was about to drift off to sleep, a thought occurred to her, and she jerked upright. Suddenly everything made sense – all the things she'd seen and heard, and her feelings, all combined into one big certainty.

"Mrrow?" Trixie enquired sleepily.

Maddie grabbed her phone and speed dialed Suzanne.

When her friend answered, Maddie blurted out, "I know who the killer is!"

***

As soon as Maddie arrived at the coffee truck the next morning, she tried calling Detective Edgewater – again. After she'd called Suzanne last night and telling her who she suspected, she'd called the sheriff's station.

But the detective wasn't on duty at that hour, although she'd been welcome to leave a message. Maddie had declined, wondering if she was doing the right thing.

She'd tossed and turned the rest of the night, Trixie finally giving up on a peaceful night and curling up on the sofa in the living room, next to *Wytchcraft for the Chosen.*

"Is he there?" Suzanne asked as Maddie waited for someone to answer the phone at the sheriff's station.

"I don't know yet."

The next second, Maddie asked for Detective Edgewater, to be told the detective was due at the station soon.

Suzanne made a face. "Maybe we should just go to the station and report your suspicions."

"Mrrow." Trixie seemed to agree with Suzanne. She sat on her stool, her ears and expression alert.

"Good idea." Maddie opened the serving window and peeked outside. "Except we have several customers waiting."

"Okay, after the early morning rush."

Maddie and Suzanne set to work, Suzanne taking the orders and the money, and Maddie making the coffee. She felt guilty at not hurrying over to the station right away, but surely another half hour before reporting her suspicions either to Detective Edgewater or the deputy on duty wouldn't hurt?

Finally, when there was only a couple of customers waiting in line, she nudged Suzanne.

"Maybe you should go over to the sheriff's station and I'll handle these regulars," Maddie suggested as she foamed milk.

"Are you sure?" Suzanne peered out of the serving hatch, pinning a smile on her face for the two regulars who waited for their coffee. "What if the—" she lowered her voice "—*killer* comes while I'm gone?"

"I should be fine." Maddie hadn't thought of that. "Trixie's here, plus there are people coming and going through the square all the time."

"True," Suzanne agreed reluctantly. "Got your cell phone on you?"

"Yes." Maddie stopped in the middle of foaming the milk and checked her pocket, making sure the phone was switched on. "In here."

"Good. Use it if you need to. I'll be as quick as I can. And try Detective Edgewater again once you've made the last latte." She nodded to the two regulars patiently waiting for their coffee. "You might be able to reach him before I do down at the station."

"Yes, boss," Maddie teased, not wanting her friend to worry. What could happen to her in the middle of the town square in broad daylight – well, eight a.m. anyway?

Suzanne departed for the sheriff's office. Maddie locked the truck door and watched her friend hurry across the town square before she returned her attention to the latte she was making.

When she gave the two customers their coffees, she sighed with relief. She might even be able to make one for herself before any more customers stepped up to the window.

Just as she was about to grind some more beans, her attention was caught by a male voice.

"Good morning, Maddie."

Walt, the newspaper reporter, stood at the counter, smiling at her.

"Hi, Walt." She attempted to sound normal, but wasn't sure if she'd succeeded. He was the last person she wanted to see right now.

"Hi Trixie," he called out to the feline. Trixie stood up straight on the stool, arching her back. Then she settled into a crouch, staring unblinkingly at him.

"She seems a bit grumpy today," he observed.

"I don't think she liked getting up early this morning," Maddie replied, hoping Trixie would understand her little fib. She had to act normal! "What can I get you?"

"How about a cappuccino?"

Maddie stared at him for a second, wondering if that was a macabre joke – it would be, if her suspicions were correct and *he was the murderer.*

When she didn't answer, he laughed. "Just kidding, Maddie. A large latte would be good."

"Sure," she replied, recovering. She finished grinding the beans, relieved to have something to occupy her trembling hands. Casting a glance over at Trixie, she was glad that the cat remained on the stool, although still in her crouched position.

When would Suzanne be back? Hopefully, with reinforcements?

But how could her friend know that she was now making coffee for a potential killer?

Her fingers brushed the pocket of her jeans that held her cell phone. If she could just get to it in time, she could try calling Detective Edgewater again. The burr and hiss of the espresso machine would help conceal the noise of the telephone call.

"I have to stay awake today," he said chattily as Maddie fiddled with the machine longer than usual, wondering if now was the time to call the detective.

But she noticed Walt's gaze on her, as if interested in the way she made his coffee. How could he fail to notice her reaching into her pocket and using her phone?

"Oh?" Maddie tried to sound interested while her heart thudded.

"I've got an interview at the radio station." He grinned. "For Dave's job. Maybe this time I'll get it."

"Good luck," she said politely, adding the foamed milk to the shots of espresso in the large cardboard cup.

"Thanks. It pays more and I really need the money right now. Mom's heart pills are more expensive than ever." He grimaced. "Not everyone can afford to pay sky high prices for medication."

Maddie froze. She forced herself to slide the latte over to him, hoping he wouldn't notice that her fingers shook. His comment was further proof that her suspicions were right. She watched as he dug into his wallet for a five-dollar bill.

"Thanks." She was careful not to let her fingers touch his as she took his money.

She gave him change, placing the coins on the serving hatch for him to pick up.

He looked a little surprised, but picked up the coins and put them in his wallet. Then he took a sip of his latte.

"You make the best coffee around," Walt complimented her. "No wonder you won the competition at the festival. I'll be sure to be a regular after this."

Maddie stared at him, aghast. That was the last thing she wanted.

"Was it something I said?" he joked, putting down the cardboard cup on the counter.

"No, it was nothing." Maddie busied herself with the machine, even though there weren't any more customers. The town square was fairly deserted, too.

"Brrrr." Trixie made a low growl in her throat.

Maddie turned to look at the cat. Trixie was still crouched on the stool, staring at Walt, but now there was a look on her face that said, *"Back off!"*

Did Trixie know that Maddie suspected Walt was the killer? Or did she somehow sense, either with her cat's intuition, or her possible witch's familiar intuition, that Walt had murdered Dave?

Maddie started as she realized Walt was peering into the truck from the serving hatch.

"Was – was there anything else?" She cleared her throat.

"You know, don't you?" His expression was now one of menace.

"Know what?" She cursed her squeaky tone.

"That I killed Dave." His hands clenched on the counter, as if he were thinking about leaping into the truck.

The hatch wasn't that big though, she tried to reassure herself. Although he was wiry, she doubted Walt could squeeze into the small space, unless he was a contortionist. But by the ugly look on his face, she wondered if adrenalin could accomplish what normal physics could not.

"Brrr." Trixie growled again.

Maddie kept one eye on the cat and one eye on Walt. Trixie's tail swished from side to side.

"I didn't say anything like that," Maddie protested.

"I could see it in your face. Right after I mentioned my mother's heart medication."

"Dave was killed by an overdose of digoxin and you mentioned heart medication," Maddie pointed out, hoping her voice didn't sound as shaky to him as it did to her.

That was what had been nagging her the whole time after their last visit to Walt at the newspaper office. The silver bracelet his mother wore in the photo on his desk was a medical alert bracelet! She'd finally realized what the engraving meant – it was the same kind of design that denoted a person had a medical condition!

"That's right." He nodded, still looking menacing. "Despite taking her expensive heart medication, Mom still needs a lot of help with everything." His face twisted. "I'd been saving to go on a cruise to the Caribbean for three years – three freaking years – but I had to give that up – as well as my apartment. I needed that money to pay for a nurse to help Mom when I'm at work. If I'd gotten the radio job two years ago, the pay rise would have been enough to help pay for her medication and the nurse. And I could have gone on that cruise."

"But Dave blackmailed one of the station executives to get the position," Maddie said softly.

"Yeah. If I'd gotten that job, I would be on that cruise ship right now, sipping mai tais and enjoying myself for once."

"Who would look after your mother?" Maddie asked, trying to keep him talking. She shot Trixie a glance – the feline still looked as if she was ready to pounce any second.

"My aunt in Colorado said she'd come and stay with Mom – she said it would be like a mini-vacation for her, and it would give her time to catch up with Mom as well. She's a lot spryer than my mother and she would have been able to manage it.

"But I had to cancel all that." His expression darkened. "And I thought I was okay with it. Until I overheard Dave the night before the festival. I was at the local bar interviewing the owner for another story, when I heard Dave boasting to someone about how he was living the good life, spending all his salary on women and alcohol and it didn't matter how much it cost because he'd just ask for another pay rise."

"And?" Maddie held her breath, hoping against hope he wasn't going to lunge at her through the serving hatch.

"That was the last straw. How dare he! I've worked my tail off all my life and now I'm living with my mother and I can't even afford to go on a vacation I saved up for – for three years!" He gave a humorless laugh. "I could barely afford that latte I just ordered from you."

Maddie took a step back.

"I took some of Mom's pills, crushed them up, mixed them with sugar in case they tasted bitter, and waited for the perfect opportunity to slip them to him. And that perfect moment occurred just as he was about to gulp down one of your cappuccinos. Someone called out to him and he put down his cup for a minute, turned around, and bingo! I'd even brought a plastic spoon with me, to make sure the powder was mixed up thoroughly in the drink." He barked a laugh.

*Escape your Enemy!* The words imprinted themselves in her mind. She cast a swift look at Trixie – the cat stared at her with glowing turquoise eyes, as if she were the one who had said those silent words and was willing Maddie to hear them.

"But everything's going to change," Walt vowed, baring his teeth. "All I have to do is take care of you and I can start my new life with my own radio show, and hire plenty of help for Mom." He paused as a thought occurred to him. "Does your friend Suzanne know, too?"

"No," Maddie replied quickly.

"I bet she does," he snarled. "I'll take care of her next."

He thrust his upper body through the serving hatch.

A sudden calmness descended on Maddie.

*"Escape my enemy*

*Escape this instant*

*Escape my enemy now!"*

Maddie quickly recited the spell three times – thank goodness she'd memorized it! There was no time to find the piece of paper with the words on it.

In the next instant in a flash of smoke and a flare of light, Maddie found herself outside the coffee truck, Trixie safely in her arms. She raced across the town square, as if she could outrun the burning sensation in her feet. Her heels felt like they were on fire! Maddie clutched Trixie to her chest, adrenalin surely making her faster than an Olympic sprinter.

A howl of outrage echoed from the coffee truck, the sound following her across the town square.

"Maddie!"

She cannoned into Suzanne, her friend's arms going around her, steadying her.

"He's in the truck," Maddie gasped, noticing Detective Edgewater standing behind her friend, his breathing rapid. "I was right. He did it!"

"Who?" The detective asked, already on his cell phone.

"Walt. The newspaper reporter."

"Mrrow!" Trixie agreed, the glow from her eyes slowly fading.

"Stay here," Detective Edgewater told them, striding over to the coffee truck.

To Maddie's surprise, there weren't many passersby around, only a couple of businessmen intent on their way to work, not taking any notice of Maddie's rush across the green expanse of lawn, or the detective hurrying over to Brewed from the Bean.

"What happened?" Suzanne asked.

Maddie rapidly filled her in, ending with, "And then I cast the Escape your Enemy spell."

"And?"

"I found myself outside the truck, Trixie in my arms. And I ran."

"Mrrow!" Trixie said, still nestled in Maddie's arms.

"So you just said the words and then the next second you were safe?"

"Sort of," Maddie replied. "There was a flash and some smoke as soon as I recited the words. And my feet," she said ruefully, twisting around to check the rear of her tennis shoes. Amazingly, they looked normal – no burn marks at all.

And, she realized, the singeing sensation had lessened to a pleasant, warm feeling in her heels.

"What about them?" Suzanne crinkled her brow.

"They felt like they were burning as soon as I found myself outside the truck. In fact—" Maddie gave a little laugh "—that feeling made me run as fast as I could."

Suzanne continued to stare at her with wide eyes. "You know," she finally said, "maybe that spell is supposed to make you feel like that."

"Mrrow," Trixie seemed to agree.

Maddie looked at Trixie and Suzanne. They both appeared to think they knew something she didn't. And then it occurred to her.

"Oh, you mean during the Salem witch trials? Or around that time? Perhaps the burning sensation is meant to warn the witch that using this spell is a lot better than being burned at the stake?" The spell book could definitely be that old.

"Yeah." Suzanne nodded, her expression serious.

Trixie snuggled further into Maddie's arms, as if that were her way of saying yes.

Maddie silently sent good wishes to anyone who had owned *Wytchcraft for the Chosen* before her, witch or not.

The reason the Escape your Enemy spell had an after-effect was sobering, especially since she hadn't experienced any with the Coffee Vision spell and the Tell the Truth spell – yet.

"We've got him." Detective Edgewater strode toward them, looking triumphant. "He started confessing as soon as I reached the truck." Behind him, two deputies accompanied Walt, who was handcuffed. He struggled between the two law enforcement officers, scowling.

"I'll need you to come down to the station later, Maddie, so you can give me your statement."

Maddie nodded, holding Trixie a little tighter as Walt passed by them. He stared straight ahead, as their presence hadn't registered at all.

Detective Edgewater cleared his throat. "I'm afraid your coffee truck is a bit of a mess." He jerked his head to the car marked Sheriff at the edge of the square. The two deputies assisted Walt into the back of the vehicle. "Walt didn't seem to like the fact that you'd escaped from the truck, and took his rage out on your coffee supplies."

Maddie closed her eyes, just imagining what she, Trixie, and Suzanne would find.

"Don't worry, Mads," Suzanne murmured. "By the time we've fixed it up, Brewed from the Bean will be good as new." Her eyes lit up. "And I bet my brother will come and help us."

"Maybe there's a spell in the book I can use," Maddie whispered in her friend's ear.

"Mrrow." Trixie looked at her approvingly, as if she'd heard the whispered words.

"I'll be down at the station." Detective Edgewater nodded to them. "We were looking at Walt as a suspect – we'd found out that he applied for the same job as Dave Dantzler two years ago. It's just our good luck and—" he grimaced "—your bad luck that he broke down at your coffee truck." He looked at them searchingly. “You didn’t invite Walt to visit your truck, did you?”

“No!” Maddie and Suzanne spoke together.

“Mrrow!” Trixie sounded cross.

“Good. This is the second murder you girls have gotten yourselves involved in – I just hope it will be your last.”

“Me too,” Maddie replied, not wanting to remember the look on Walt’s face when he’d realized she knew he was the killer.

Maddie and Detective Edgewater both looked at Suzanne.

“We can’t help it if suspects talk to us,” she declared. As the detective frowned at her, she added, “But as soon as Maddie realized who the killer was, she tried to contact you. And so did I.”

Maddie nodded. “But you weren’t at the station,” she told the detective.

He flushed. “Next time leave a message and ask them to contact me straight away. I don’t want anything to happen to you two—” he looked over at Trixie “—three.”

“Us either,” Suzanne put in.

He furrowed his brow as he looked at Maddie. “How did you and Trixie get out of the truck, anyway? When the deputies got there, they had to force the door – it was locked from the inside – to reach Walt.”

“Magic,” Suzanne said airily, waving her hand in the air.

“Yeah, right.” The detective shook his head as he walked toward his vehicle. “Come by the station this afternoon to give your statement, Miss Goodwell - Maddie.”

The three of them watched the vehicle pull away from the curb.

“Suzanne,” Maddie scolded her friend, “you can’t tell anyone—”

“I know.” Suzanne smiled. “And that was the only time I’ve ever mentioned the M word to anyone, apart from you – and Trixie. But it worked, didn’t it?”

“Mrrow,” Trixie agreed, nudging Suzanne’s arm.

Suzanne obliged, stroking the cat held securely in Maddie’s arms.

“Detective Edgewater will be too busy to wonder how you got out of a locked truck, and you’ll be too busy to do anything else apart from preparing for the Seattle competition next month, dating my brother, and seeing if there are any other spells in the book you can cast – like a tidy up spell for the truck. That would be awesome!"

"And what are you going to do while I'm busy with all that?" Maddie asked.

"Having another massage with Ramon, coming up with new health ball recipes – and oh yeah, making sure you win the big Seattle competition next month."

***

I hope you enjoyed reading this mystery. To discover when the next Maddie Goodwell mystery will be released, please sign up to my newsletter at: www.JintyJames.com

Have you read:

Spells and Spiced Latte – A Coffee Witch Cozy Mystery – Maddie Goodwell 1

Magic and Mocha – A Coffee Witch Cozy Mystery – Maddie Goodwell 3

Enchantments and Espresso – A Coffee Witch Cozy Mystery – Maddie Goodwell 4

Jinty James grew up reading Enid Blyton's Famous Five and Secret Seven mysteries, as well as all the Nancy Drew and Trixie Belden books. Later on, she graduated to mysteries written by Agatha Christie, Elizabeth Peters, and many other authors. It was her dream to one day write her own cozy mystery, and now she has, with plans for many more.

## Maple Macadamia Health Ball Recipe

USA Measurements:

¾ cup pitted dates
½ cup shelled, raw macadamias
2 Tablespoons maple syrup
1½ Tablespoons shredded or desiccated coconut

**NOTES:**

- There might still be little bits of crunchy macadamia in the balls, even after lots of whizzing in the food processor.
- The balls might be a bit sticky to touch even covered in coconut.
- These balls are best eaten on the day you make them.

**METHOD:**

Whiz the dates, macadamias, and maple syrup in a food processor as finely as possible. Roll into small balls.

Place the coconut on a plate and roll the balls into the coconut, then refrigerate for one hour to set.

Makes 7 balls.

**Maple Macadamia Health Ball Recipe**

METRIC MEASUREMENTS:

105g pitted dates
47g shelled, raw macadamias
30 mls maple syrup
1½ Tablespoons (22.5mls) shredded or desiccated coconut

**NOTES:**

- There might still be little bits of crunchy macadamia in the balls, even after lots of whizzing in the food processor.
- The balls might be a bit sticky to touch even covered in coconut.
- These balls are best eaten on the day you make them.

**METHOD:**

Whiz the dates, macadamias, and maple syrup in a food processor as finely as possible. Roll into small balls.

Place the coconut on a plate and roll the balls into the coconut, then refrigerate for one hour to set.

Makes 7 balls.

Made in United States
North Haven, CT
03 January 2024